ALSO BY MARTHA TOD DUDMAN

Expecting to Fly

Augusta, Gone

MARTHA TOD DUDMAN

*Black
Olives*

A NOVEL

simon & schuster
new york   london   toronto   sydney

SIMON & SCHUSTER
Rockefeller Center
1230 Avenue of the Americas
New York, NY 10020

First Simon & Schuster hardcover edition February 2008

SIMON & SCHUSTER and colophon are registered trademarks of Simon & Schuster, Inc.

For information about special discounts for bulk purchases,
please contact Simon & Schuster Special Sales at
1-800-456-6798 or business@simonandschuster.com

Designed by Karolina Harris

Manufactured in the United States of America

10   9   8   7   6   5   4   3   2   1

Library of Congress Cataloging-in-Publication Data
Dudman, Martha Tod.
  Black olives : a novel / Martha Tod Dudman.—1st Simon & Schuster hardcover ed.
        p. cm.
  1. Single women—Fiction. 2. Separation (Psychology)—Fiction. I. Title.
PS3604.U37B57 2008
813'.6—dc22

                              2007012949

ISBN: 978-1-4165-4961-1

Black
Olives

1

Nine months later, I run into David for the first time since our breakup. All year I've been dreading this moment, but always dressing in expectation of it, because when I do see him, finally, I want to look good.

I'm standing in Rogerson's Emporium, over by the olives, when it happens. I hear the door open and I glance around and see him walking in. I recognize at once the bright flag of his white hair, but I've got my back to him and he doesn't notice me.

This feeling goes through me, like my cell phone's on vibrate and it's going off in my pocket—like I'm experiencing a minor electric shock. Like I can't move. Maybe he won't see me. Won't recognize the back of my head, the jacket I'm wearing, the once familiar shape of my ass.

Is she with him? I crane around, but I don't see a woman near him. He's alone.

I turn back to the refrigerated case. The black olives there are so shiny, in their little plastic containers. I want to distract myself with olives, to think about olives; the various colors and textures, degrees of saltiness.

There are other people in the store but they don't count. I am aware only of him. He walks over to the place where they grind the coffee and asks for Samoan. I can hear him right across the store. It's the first time I've heard his voice in nine months, after hearing it every day for ten years.

I stare down at the olives. There are little white cards above the olive containers, printed in a definite black hand. I wonder if the saleswoman in the white smock wrote them. The olives are described generously, romantically, as if they were wines, or "Staff Picks" in a book shop: *meaty, luscious, mild. Tart, intriguing. Try these with a dry white wine.* Everything is unreal.

"Can I help you?"

The woman in the white smock with the wide, wholesome face, and the unfortunate, dumpy cook's hat, is smiling at me.

I imagine that she knows, and the other woman, the one cutting the roast beef, knows, and the man in the brown coat examining the gourmet mustards, he knows—they all know—about the drama taking place in their store.

They all know that I—the woman by the olives—was abandoned nine months ago by the man who is purchasing Samoan coffee, oblivious to my proximity.

Will I speak to him? Will I flounce by? Will I hide from him?

For nine months I have imagined this meeting. I have rehearsed all the sad things, the reproachful things, the angry things I have to say to him. The words of sorrow and revenge. The words of fury. But now, here in Rogerson's Emporium, I am mute. I want only to turn to the woman in the frumpy hat and rest my head against her crisp, white-smocked bosom and cry.

I feel as if I could cry forever. I could begin crying right here by the olives. My eyes might wander as they blur, over the fancy

mint pastilles, the dried nectarines, the chocolate-covered ginger slices. I might observe the fancy jellies in their square glass
jars—the shape of the jars somehow implying privilege—and
these things would all seem meaningless, like foreign objects,
like conversations full of words that I don't understand—and
then, finally, I would give myself over to my enormous sorrow,
and fling myself like a little child onto that smooth white smock
and cry and cry and cry—the snotty, noisy, fulfilling kind of cry
a child cries—heedless, unending, and final. The tears of all the
year gone by.

The woman behind the counter looks at me curiously. Maybe
she has asked me a question.

"No, thank you," I say just in case, whispering, because I don't
want David to hear my voice, to turn around, to look at me. I'm
not ready yet. Nine months and I'm still not ready. How should
I handle this?

I glance back again, over my shoulder. He still has his back to
me. He hasn't seen me. This is still my show. I've rehearsed it so
often but now, faced with the moment, I hesitate. I feel so shy
with the man I once knew inside out. The man I spoke to every
day for ten years, the man I slept with, now a stranger.

I look blindly at the lady in the white smock, as if she might
have some good advice, and the lady looks back at me, thinking
whatever she thinks.

I can't speak to him, here, in Rogerson's Emporium, ye phony
old grocery store. Not here amid the fine wines and the dilly
beans and cheese straws.

I step quietly over, positioning myself behind the shelves, and peer around at him. Is he as tall as he used to be? Doesn't he look different somehow? But he's wearing a sweater that I remember putting my face against.

It's too much. I can't be the jaunty girl I want to be; say something glib yet cutting—apparently kind, but with a sharp knife edge, the dagger that you notice later—*what have we here?*—while the blood runs down. I can't think of what to say, what to do. I just want to squeeze around the espresso machines and licorice whips, get out that door, and escape.

And now, as I crouch by the various honeys and chutneys of life, it's as if everyone else in the store is frozen, like one of those scenes in a movie where only two of the actors move and all the rest are completely still. Like that romantic scene in *West Side Story,* where Tony and Maria meet at the dance. The other actors all look like they're made out of wood or wax or some other inanimate substance, not human flesh.

They're all motionless: the woman in the funny hat who looks like a librarian; the ponderous older couple cruising the wines; the elfin, thin man with his complimentary paper cup of Ecuadorian coffee; the lady by the salsas; the bearded man who roasts the coffee and measures it out into the tall white paper bags. All of them irrelevant and stilled. It is only the two of us—David and I—only we two—who are alone alive in the vast store silence.

He starts to turn and I duck back behind the shelves again. From here I can see his feet on the wooden floor. He's wearing the shoes he always wears. A certain kind of walking shoe that he favors, brown leather Rockports. I work my way along the span of shelving, as he on the far side, still unaware of me, moves toward the cheese.

I'll wait until he's occupied, then make a dash for it, as if I were engaged in some long-ago schoolyard game on an asphalt field. I was never much good at kickball. When I was occasionally, by some trick of fate, catapulted onto the bases, I felt very proud and self-conscious. The cheering around me like silence. Ready to run.

And now I will run—out from behind the tall shelf full of pickles and marinades. I will make a dash for the door and rush through it. He won't have a chance to see me; I will just be a blur.

Only, maybe he will. He will cry out to me, come after me, follow me into the parking lot pleading *come back to me come back to me* because finally, this time, for once, *I* will be the one who has left.

I dart out from behind the shelves, knock against a tall cappuccino mug (bright red) that teeters, but, amazingly, I catch it backhanded without stopping, yank open the door, and slam out into the parking lot, breathing hard. The door falls shut behind me. Did he see me? I'm afraid to look.

2

Outside, it is a blissful autumn day. The golden light of September and the green leaves still full; cars going by on Main Street and the sound of the river heading toward the sea. The parking lot is cluttered with bright cars, which all seem new, fresh-washed and shiny in the sunshine. My own car: dark blue, the moonroof open, and red leather seats. And there, almost beside it, only one car over, is his Jeep Cherokee. Black and shiny, with the loon license plates. He's always pretended and longed to be a Mainer, instead of what he is—a guy from Philadelphia who moved here in the nineties.

Didn't he see my car when he pulled in? Wouldn't he have noticed? Because I would have, if I were the one who pulled in and his car was there. For nine months I've been driving around expecting to see him, longing to see him, afraid of seeing him, eyeing each black truck I pass. Hasn't he done that, too—looked for my blue car, expected my pale face in every reflecting, flashing windshield that passed him by?

I've got to get out of here. He could come out any moment. This isn't how I want to see him, where I want to see him—after all this time. I want the moment when I see him to be carefully choreographed. I want to be the one who decides the time and the place. I've imagined many different scenarios, but it's never been like this—a sunny parking lot, cars going by, the dusty sunlit stillness of the asphalt, an ordinary September afternoon.

The triumphant, confrontational scenes that I've imagined have all taken place in much more flattering light, for one thing. Dim restaurants, for example. I with a handsome man of some sort, and David, of course, alone. I striding, tall and powerful in sexy heels. He slumped down in a booth, regretful, rueful, beaten down by life, ashamed. In my invented dreams he's always been the one who's startled, routed from his ruminations, and I am in control.

I say hello, somewhat grandly, though kind—I would be kind, I think—looming over him, imperious, elegant, perfectly coifed.

David! I say.

He stares at me, transfixed. He'd forgotten my beauty. The sheer power of my magnetic presence.

Virginia? he says, dully. *How are you?*

Oh, I'm wonderful! My voice is clear and confident. Then, softly, and with concern, I ask, *Are you all right?* because he looks so ill.

He mumbles something, looks away, ashamed, and I move on.

There are other versions, of course, honed in those still and silent center hours of the night. Other versions, but in each one I am triumphant, proud, victorious, and noble. In none of them am I standing in a parking lot, having fled in fearful haste at the sight of him.

No, this won't do at all.

I look back at Rogerson's Emporium, but the door's still shut. I start walking across the parking lot, noticing every detail the way you notice every single little thing when you're as charged as I am—the shiny cars, the dusty grayness of the asphalt, the faded parking lines worn out by summer, the full, bright beauty of the sky above downtown Sinclair—those tight brick buildings and the round bank clock!

I walk fast across the parking lot and along the sidewalk to the bridge, and don't look back once. So what if he sees me? I almost *want* him to see me. Finally, after all this time, all these months and months—nine months! enough to have a baby! enough months to complete a school year!—we should just see each other and get it over with. Then maybe I can have some peace. Maybe I can stop thinking about him the way I've been thinking about him all year. Going over and over the last months that we were together: thinking what I could have done differently; what I did do; how it ended.

I get to the middle of the bridge, stop, and lean over. The bright water is rushing down below, rushing toward the sea, and the wind's against me. I feel like I'm on top of a big boat with the full, hard breeze on my face. I stare down into the white plumy water, and then, of course, I can't help imagining what I look like standing here—what he'd see if he came out right now and saw me with my hair, newly dyed a sort of mahogany color, shining dramatically in the sunshine with its reddish lights and my bright skirt flying against my legs. I'm glad, at least, I'm wearing the right shoes.

I make a wish or a prayer or something, staring into the river. *Let me be done with this. Let me just see him. Let me get straight with him. Let me get over him. It's enough. It's enough. It's enough.*

I scrinch my eyes shut to give my wish more power, cars rushing by behind me. The woman alone on the bridge.

But, okay. So now what?

He still hasn't come out. He still hasn't seen me. What can he be doing in there? I can't just wait here on the bridge all afternoon. None of this is working out the way I planned. That's the problem, isn't it, with involving more than one person in a fantasy? I walk back quickly to the parking lot. I'll get in my car and drive home. This won't be the time that I see him, after all. I'll do something—I don't know—clean out a closet or something, rewrite my will. It's Saturday afternoon, a good day for getting things done.

I'm just about to get into my car, when I suddenly turn around, like somebody's making me do it, and walk over to his Jeep. It's like I can't help myself. I stick my head in the open window, and feel the warm interior air against my face.

The back seat's full of junk as usual. Behind the driver's seat I can see the rubble of his life—the bright yellow foul weather jacket, the black fleece vest, a couple of sweaters. The air inside the truck is warm and familiar. I can smell him.

Something happens to me at that moment. It's all like a dream—the smell of the truck, the warm air. I don't even know what I'm doing; I just open the door of the truck and I get in, as if I had planned it—climb right into the back, into that odd cluttery space where there's an old winter parka, a half-empty pretzel box. I burrow down into the folds of his sweaters, pull something over myself, and snuggle down.

Beyond the cave of my making I can hear the cars passing by on Main Street. I am warm and sleepy. Lully. I'm not really thinking about anything. It's so cozy. After a little bit, I sit up and gulp in the good clean air that comes in through the open window, but then, across the parking lot, I see the door to Rogerson's open. My heart starts beating faster. I peer out, still mostly hidden, but no, it's someone else going to another car: two old people with their bags. I hunker back down, hear their car door open, shut, the car drive off. Then silence.

I lie down again, listen to the cars and the sound of the river. And then, without warning, the truck door opens and David climbs in, throws something in the back on top of me. I can hear the crunchy sound the bag makes as it lands. I can hear him breathing. He just sits there for a moment without moving. Did he notice my car just one car over? It's on his right side, so maybe not. Does he know I'm here? Can he smell me? I lie as still as I can. Neither one of us moving. Cars, bag on my back, and his breathing.

Why doesn't he get going? Why doesn't he just start the truck already? Does he know I'm back here, hidden right behind his seat? Is he deciding what to say to me?

I'm starting to get a little panicky feeling. I'm about to get caught. How will I explain this? What was my plan, exactly, when I crawled in here?

Should I reveal myself to him? Should I rise up behind him—appear in his rearview mirror—a ghost from his past? Would he be frightened, shocked? Or does he already know I'm here? Is he just being quiet to torture me a little before he says something? *What are you doing back there?*

What's the point of this, Virginia?

There *is* no point, I realize. I'm starting to get that twitchy feeling you get when you stay still too long. But what can I do? There is no way to salvage this moment. I'll just have to wait until he gets out.

But what if he's making a long trip somewhere? Driving to Indiana, for example. Going to Rockland, or New York? I could be in here for days.

Weeks later he'll notice a peculiar smell in the Jeep. He'll think nothing of it at first. Maybe old socks. Stale winter boots. My decomposing body stuffed down in the back. Dank with urine. Suffocated under the rubble. And then he'll be sorry, I bet.

He's still sitting there motionless in the driver's seat. Does he know I'm back here? Did he see me from the windows of Rogerson's? Is he waiting for me to do something? Can he hear my heart? Is he listening to me breathe? I want to stop breathing, but I can't. My breath seems enormous, deafening: my big, loud, inappropriate breathing. I am huffing and puffing back here under the Irish fisherman's sweater my father once gave him. *He's just like a son to me,* my dad told me. *Seems like part of the family,* my mother said. And he was.

He knows I'm here. He knows what I'm thinking. He's waiting for me to do something. Thinking up something to say.

Suddenly he's just going to speak. He'll say my name. He will say it in that teacher voice he gets sometimes. So stern and prissy.

Virginia, he'll say, *how long are you planning to stay back there?*

He will try to sound amused, but he will not be entirely amused. This is, after all, a sort of breaking and entering, isn't it? I have broken and entered his truck. Isn't that sort of like entering somebody's house? That's the sort of question I used to ask him, back when he was my boyfriend. *Would that count as a crime?* I would have asked him, and he would look serious, thinking it over, and I would think how nice it was to have such a serious boyfriend who knew these big facts.

I don't know what his life is like now. I used to know every detail of it. I used to know everything he did, where he went, what he ate. We talked on the phone every day, sometimes two or three times a day. I knew the colors of his socks, the book he was reading, the texture of his days. I knew him by heart for ten years and he me, and now, only nine months later, I know nothing at all. I don't even know if he still lives in the same house. Don't know if he eats at Donegal's, or stopped going there, afraid that he might see me. Don't know if he still goes to Bob's Lunch to drink his coffee, read his newspaper, check out the girls. Don't know if he has a new jacket or still wears that mossy green one he bought to please me. I don't know if he has a girlfriend, or several girlfriends. If he still has the photographs of me which he used to have all over the house. *I like to see you in every room,* he told me once. *I like to look up and see your face.* The photograph by his desk—of me in that flowered dress taken one spring morning outside my office. I was only forty years old. *I love that picture of you,* he used to say. I knew that he meant he loved me.

I think of this now, stuffed in the back of the Jeep, with him motionless in the front seat, waiting to hear the doom of his voice.

Why doesn't he just say something and get it over with? Why doesn't he just say my name?

And then I would come out of my crampy small place and admit all my craziness.

But he doesn't do anything. Doesn't say anything, so I just stay where I am, squeezed down.

And then, just when I think I can stand it no longer, I will have to sneeze, or scratch or shout or do something—anything—he starts the engine. Here we are, we are on our way. There's no turning back now.

3

He backs out quickly, and there's this gravelly sound. Pulls up with a jerk to the edge of the parking lot, ready to drive out into the streaming cars of Main Street headed east to the coast or west to the hills beyond.

He turns on the radio, a little too loud. Is he losing his hearing? Already in nine months he's gone deaf? And what's he listening to, anyway? Alan Jackson? Since when does he like country music? He definitely has a new girlfriend. He would never do this on his own. *If life were like the movies. Don't rock the jukebox.* Ah.

He seems to be humming along. It's weird to be this close to him after all this time; separated only by the back of the seat—a few inches of metal, the seat cushions, our individual clothes. I remember how close we used to sit—pressed close together, on the couch, on a walk, in the bed. How I could feel the reassuring pressure of him close by. The time my neighbors, the Quimbys, dropped by when David and I had been making love in the afternoon. We'd just put our clothes back on and were coming downstairs to nose around in the kitchen, find something to eat. I had that gangly, stupid, loose-limbed feeling. Post-love. I haven't felt like that in a long time now—that lovely feeling of being given over to pleasure and combined by it into one.

We were just coming down the stairs in our socks when we

heard the thumpy, alien Quimby tread on the front steps. Then the door opening. "Yoo hoo! Virginia?" *The neighbors!*

We stopped on the stairs, stared at each other in horror, then asked them in and offered them tea and cookies, though we'd both wanted to tear into the remains of last night's chicken that stood on its blue-and-white plate in the fridge. We sat on the long green couch where we'd gotten started an hour before. We were pressed side to side, close together, sitting there like two ducks, staring at the Quimbys, wondering if they knew, if they could smell it on us—the sweet, salty smell of sex. Mr. Quimby in his Sunday sport jacket and khaki pants. Mrs. Quimby with her L.L.Bean denim jumper and her heavy brown New Balance walking shoes.

"Nice people," David said when they were finally gone. "I thought they'd never leave."

And then, both of us, rueful and giggly, falling back on the couch together. How in love we were! And how long it lasted! All of it.

The feel of his body against mine in the bed, on the couch, in the kitchen, where we stood close together, arms around one another, hugging and hugging. The firm pressure of his stomach against mine; reassuring and adult and solid. The feeling of my breasts against his chest. How amazed I was at the sheer fact of him at first—to have a lover at last after all those years. To be now at forty, at forty-five, so startled and stunned by love—when I'd thought I was done with all that. To spend all afternoon with the sun across my face lying in a wilderness of sheets and wrinkled blankets—to look across the room at the mirror on the back of the bedroom door and see the two of us—two survivors surviving together, having made it through bad marriages, bad love affairs, all the disasters and disappointments of life—having swum to this farther shore and discovered each other.

How I loved him! How I deplored him! How he irritated, bored, annoyed me sometimes. How he delighted me. How we became like siblings. How we squabbled. But still, at the movies, on our walks together, what I remember is touch: his hand in my hand, his arm around me, holding the soft part of my upper arm as we walked. His hands on my body in darkness. How he'd just be there, take me to him, hold me. How I felt so safe.

And now, wedged in here in the back, tucked under the hot sweater, hoping I don't sneeze—and just thinking I might makes me want to—I am reminded of all of it. I can hear his tuneless humming, up there with the radio on, and I am back here, alone, but so close. But for these few inches, I could touch him now.

We are bumping along down the road. I don't know which way. Can't tell, by the pull and switch of the truck, if we are going north or south, east or west. I think I might even fall asleep back here, lulled by the motion. I've been so tired for so long—for months it seems like—and there's nothing I can do, for now, but lie here. Lie here and be close to him. Is that what I want most of all?

•••

I don't know what you want, I wrote him once in an e-mail. But that was later, after things had soured.

At first it was almost undetectable. We still did the things that we did. We still talked on the phone every day; we still went out to dinner. We still went on our walks together, with his arm around me. But something was different. It was like a rotten smell that you smell when you first come into the house. A mouse that has died in the cabinet? Some old food that someone forgot to throw out? You smell it when you first walk in and you say, *What's that smell?* and wrinkle up your nose, but then you check the answering machine and your e-mails and you go up and change your clothes and gradually you forget that the smell's even there.

He told me last fall that he was depressed. He'd been grumpy, abstracted. He was trying to sell his company, a deal he'd been negotiating for years. A deal I was beginning to think might never happen, though I kept encouraging him, kept telling him to hang in there, that he was doing the right thing. Imagined with him the trip we'd take together when the business was finally sold. To Italy. To Portugal. Somewhere with bright sun and bleached houses. Who does he travel with now?

I would often catch him staring at me.

"What?" I'd say playfully, because in the old days that stare meant we would make love.

But not anymore. We never made love anymore, except a sort of halfway, unhappy love. He touched me but then wasn't able to follow through. He didn't want to talk about it. There was some mysterious thing with his prostate that he wouldn't discuss.

I would have done anything to bring him back to me, but he wouldn't talk about it. He would just stop, then lie there silently, angrily, as if it were my fault.

"What is it?" I asked on one of those nights, and reached out to him, hoping to salvage the situation. Still wanting him, even though I was angry at him. The memory of the body is so strong. His hands were the hands I knew, and I wanted him. His touch. His smell. His mouth on my body. My skin felt hot. I rolled toward him, "What is it?"

But he lay there mute. He hated for me to mention it. Hated it here in the bed; grew sullen and silent.

Don't talk about sexual dysfunction, erectile dysfunction, when you're in bed with your husband, the ladies' magazine at my gynecologist's office advised. *Find some neutral place to discuss your sexual life.* But he also hated talking about it when we were not in the bed, if I brought it up on a walk. If I dared to mention it on the phone so he wouldn't have to look at me. All of these things he hated and hated. Sometimes I thought what he really hated was me.

And oh, how he wanted me once!

I wanted to tear your clothes off when I saw you standing there in that skirt of yours, he used to tell me.

I wanted to throw you down on the bed.

How we twisted together—once!

But now, in the morning, in the still, grayish light of the bed-room, I slipped out of the bed hoping he was not yet awake. Glad he was not wearing his glasses. Let me be blurred and un-real, so he will not see how I've aged.

I wanted to get my robe on and get out of the room, before he saw me. Before he could see what he'd discarded, what he no longer wanted. My breasts ridiculous at fifty. My ass. My belly. All full of shame, because he no longer wanted me.

I was no longer forty. I was fifty. I felt lined and puckered. Ev-erything sliding downward. My aging felt inevitable and un-stoppable and unfair. And it was accelerated by his disdain.

At forty I had still seemed to myself to be nearly invincible. But now, at fifty, I realized that this would continue—this sad, slow descent.

We are descending now. Going downhill, I can feel it. The Jeep jouncing. Maybe it's a dirt road? Or has the road to his place gotten more full of potholes? Has it gotten this old and worn already in the nine months since we were together?

I still remember that morning and my embarrassed, crablike scuttle to the bathroom, when I grabbed my robe off the hook and hurried out. We had our wake-up showers and familiar morning conversation, the toast, the newspaper, the juice, the coffee—all of these things that separated us from the sorrowful bedroom—and we were brought into the happy day.

It was Sunday in Bentonville: the farmer's market with its tables full of plump, end-of-the-season tomatoes, so red and with their dusty, spicy-smelling vines, dirt brown potatoes, and the last flowers of the season, more vivid than any all summer long. The parking lot was full of surly, bearded, organic farmers with their ugly hats and wistful women in their droopy skirts. Jars of preserves. The endless loaves of bread; their whole wheat domes. We saw various people that we knew: Diana from my women's group with her surprisingly handsome husband—*Where'd she get him?*—a lady from the bank, a local lawyer. David bought me herbs to make up for the sex: a bunch of basil, a bag of apples— "We can split them." "Okay."—another sad reminder of our apartness—he in his house and I in mine, each eating our lonely apples far apart. At sixty he wanted a wife. He said that again and again. But I liked our separate houses, our separate lives.

It was the bag of apples, I thought later, that might have done it. Maybe before that there was a chance. Maybe it was the division of the apples, that sad arithmetic, that divided us forever, that made him so angry.

I'm so angry all the time, he said that last night.

Well, he doesn't sound angry now, whistling away up front in his truck, crooning along with Alan Jackson, his voice coming in on the chorus. *Don't rock the jukebox.* Blah blah. I rumbling along in the back, well hidden. Waiting it out.

...

Then that day—what else was there? Brunch at Tree Dog with the Sunday *Times.* He had the eggs with feta. I had a sweet roll—one of those gooey, heavy ones with lots of nuts. *Don't you want some protein?* No and no. I wanted something sweet. Always in those days I wanted something sweet. A little piece of dense, dark chocolate after a salty, meaty meal. A cup of cocoa. Ice cream in a cone. Butter pecan or cherries jubilee. Jelly on my toast. Funny that later, when he was gone, those things would so repel me.

Now chocolate seemed like a dark abomination in my belly. I'd loved it once so much. Meat. Sausages. Bacon. All the daring dark carcinogens I used to love now seemed so terrible to me. I didn't eat. It seemed as if I didn't eat all winter. Got thin and thinner. Stood sideways to the mirror and tried to please my solitary self with hip bones. With how thin I got. Size eight. Size six. How thin and yet much thinner. But so what? Without him there.

But back then—the *New York Times* and feta cheese! Chopped tomato and bright green scallion in the eggs. *Try this, it's so good! What is that, basil?* We made up funny little stories about the other people there. We made up funny little stories and we pretended that everything was all right, that this was one of the mornings we'd been making love, that we were young again, or almost young. That we were in the first happy days of our affair and not in the sad, last, lost ones.

I thought we could reach through that. *A bad patch* he used to call it. And I believed that we would make it through again. The way we had before.

And after all the feta and the Style section me and he the Sports I suggested a walk. "Want to walk on that path we like?"

That path we liked. The many paths we liked. The paths along the shore, the one along the river. The path behind my house through the woods that led up to the top of the little mountain, the miniature mountain with the flat stone top where I used to take my children for picnics when they were very little. When I think now of how it was back then it all seems lit by another light. Back then when the children were younger and we were in love.

4

We walked through the sunny woods that day on a path that was sometimes wide enough for the two of us, sometimes too narrow. He walked ahead and I observed his shaggy white hair, his broad back, and his behind in his old man jeans. How he'd changed. Gotten stringier and stingier and older. His face more lined. His eyebrows wilder. His eyes more sunken. But still I loved him. Those changes in him made me feel protective of him, tender. He was my man.

We walked a ways in silence. It felt like a good silence. We'd had our eggs. The day was perfect. The sunshine made me optimistic: surely we could get through whatever this was, to some other place on the other side of it where we would be happy together. *Talk things through* the articles said in that women's magazine way.

"David," I began.

"Yes, Virginia."

"David, how come we don't make love anymore?"

I didn't want to use the word *erection*. Such a terrible, pointy, cruel edifice of a word.

He walked on beside me, didn't speak.

"Are you having an affair or something?" I asked him. I knew he wasn't, but shouldn't I ask?

"Of course not," he said. Then: "Do you really want to know?"

"Not if it's going to hurt my feelings."

"You hurt my feelings lots of times, Virginia."

"I know. I'm sorry." I answered very low.

"Sometimes you turn away from me when I go to kiss you. Sometimes I feel like I'm just an encumbrance in your life.

"I don't know, Virginia. This is a rough patch. I feel as if you're too busy for me. And then I've got a lot on my mind. Trying to sell the business. Get that settled. The kids. The real estate."

So it wasn't *all* my fault, but sort of, mostly. My fault for being too busy. My fault for being too ambitious. My fault for turning away. My fault about the erection, lack of erection, lack of love between us, sourness and dust.

But then, that wasn't right. It wasn't all my fault. Okay, well maybe a little, maybe half. But not my fault that he couldn't get it up! That wasn't fair! I thought. And then I remembered when I'd heard all this before—five years ago when we were going through another *rough patch* and he didn't want to make love to me. And my dad was sick. David had complained that I was too busy. Well, yes, I was pretty busy. Busy going to the hospital. Busy driving in a fog of pain. Busy trying to keep it all together for my mother, for my children. Busy busy busy. Too busy to be the kind of girlfriend he required.

And I had neglected him. Abandoned him for my own dark pain. But wasn't it different now? In the past years, since my dad was well, and the kids were grown and then gone off to college, I had tried so hard to make things better. And oh how

I hate that *working* term people use about love—as if love were some big hole you had to dig or rocks you had to carry from one place to another. Only maybe it is.

But I did try, I did work, hating the word, hating the slog of it, but knowing that I wanted him, that he was important to me in my life. I did try. Made space for him, a little space in all my clutter. Cooked for him. Spent time with him. Went to his house with its sad odor of neglect and loneliness. Took vacations with him. Made love to him. Lost weight for him. I exercised to bring him back to me. Bought new underwear that I found slightly embarrassing and inappropriate for someone my age, but which I wore to woo him. All of the truck and trifle of seduction. I had tried, and somehow we had patched the bad patch back together, gotten over the rough place, and gone on.

And here we were again, in the sunny woods, trying to sort out our life. I felt guilty, because I always felt a little guilty, but I knew it wasn't all my fault.

"You know what," I said, stopping suddenly, turning to look right at him. The sun warm on my face, the piney smell of the woods all around. "I don't think that's right. That used to be right. I used to do that. But it's not right now. That's not what's wrong. I've been really nice. I've been trying."

He bowed his head. Didn't look at me. "Yeah. You have been trying."

Then he got that look he sometimes got. Stubborn in a sort of sullen way. "You try. But I always feel I come last in your life, Virginia. You don't have time for me."

"I have time for you," but I said it less certainly now. *Did I?*

There were so many times when he called and I saw his name on the caller ID and there was this feeling that went through me—this sort of wash of a feeling, a gray wash—*Oh. So that's who it is—ringing my phone. Calling me up. Wanting to talk to me. Him*—right before I clicked the button that brought his weary voice to me, the voice that I imagined welling up, swelling up from his cellar or deeper than that, from some subterranean pit: his own dark depths. I always pictured him there, though of course he wasn't. Pictured him as if I were looking down at him, down a long deep tunnel to where he was below. Though he wasn't, of course. Most of the time when he called me he was at his desk in his study, or in his kitchen. I would ask, "Where are you?" and he would say, "I'm in the kitchen." "I'm at my desk." But somehow I always imagined him in his cellar, that musty, stuffy swamp of old shoes and mold spores. His lonely bachelor divorced man laundry heaped on the dryer to iron. Last winter's jackets hung on the hooks like the pelts of old animals. His son's old navy blue parka. The boots of the lost boys. The unused workbench. The bags and bags and bags of bottles to be recycled. The bundles of old newspapers, ditto. The smell of stale beer, old *Bangor Daily News,* and old *Times.*

That's where I imagined him standing, swaying slightly from side to side the way he did, phone to his ear, calling me with nothing whatsoever to say.

"Yeah?" I would ask him.

"Oh, I just called," he would say. Waiting for me to do the

work of our conversations. Waiting for my adventures with clients, my plans for us. Had I made reservations for dinner somewhere? Was there a party? Did I hear some splendid bit of gossip or was I full of some drama of my own? That's what he called for. He called to hear my voice. He called to hear my stories. He called to touch me. He was lonely there, in his cellar or not in his cellar. He was lonely in his life. And he thought that I would somehow change that, save him, give him something—some juice, some warmth, some light.

The truth is, I often didn't want to take his call. Knowing it was a call about nothing. Knowing it was a call, not for conversation, but for life. I felt drained by him. Drained and then drained again by his depression, by his endless need. By his always wanting wanting wanting something from me that he just couldn't seem to ever really get.

And he, in turn, was furious with me. Furious and abandoned. He felt abandoned. Though we went on our dates once a week, though he stayed over at my house, or I at his, though I called him up to ask how the doctor appointment went, if he needed anything when he was sick—and he was sick so often!—if he wanted to join me at dinner at one of my events. None of this was what he wanted. He wanted me there in his house living with him. And the thought of it sickened me and made me feel dead inside; made me feel strangled.

I remembered the stories he'd told me about the last ten years of his twenty-year marriage. Lying in bed beside his wife. Not touching, hating to hear her breathe. I remember how horrible it sounded. How they would sit in the evening in different rooms each with their own book reading, reading, hearing the sound of the page turning in the other room where the other one sat. Unable to stand even being in the same room together.

"What did you do?" I'd ask him.

"I don't know. Watched a game on television. Went out for a walk. Walked the dog. Sometimes I'd go drive around, just drive around after work. I'd go down to the shore and just sit there in my truck and stare at the water."

"Why didn't you get a divorce? Why didn't one of you leave?"

"I don't know. The kids, I guess."

The kids, I guess. I never could have stood it. Ten years of it. Eternity.

"Was it ever good?"

"Oh, sure," he told me. "It was good in the beginning. In the beginning, when we were in love."

"What happened, though? She was nice, wasn't she? She was pretty."

"Oh, yeah, she was nice. She was pretty. She was great. She could be mean though."

That's all he had. *She could be mean.* Well, who couldn't?

He'd had affairs when he was married. He had told me that.

"Did she know?"

"I don't know. I don't think so."

"I bet she did," I told him. "Whether she knew out loud or just in the back of her mind, I bet she knew."

He shrugged. "I don't know. It was a long time ago."

Somehow he believed it would be different if he were married to me. That he would be finally happy, with me in his house.

But I didn't think so. I thought of his old marriage, of the stories he had told me, remembered my own sullen little marriage, the short time it lasted, and thought no. No, I could never live with this man. We would come to hate one another in days. In minutes. Him with his breathing. Him with his trips to the bathroom, newspaper in hand. Lumping off to the toilet for a good read, for a good long session on the throne with the crossword puzzle, or his book on the Civil War. His slippers with the trodden-down sides. His shirts piled up on the dryer. Would he want me to iron them for him? Probably. Or else he would do it himself, but he would iron them in a reproachful way, as if it should have been me all along ironing those shirts.

And it wasn't just that. How about the talking? How about having to talk to somebody else all the time—to have him always right there? Prowling around when I was reading my book. Tromping up and down the stairs.

Oh, marriage. All wrong for everybody! Or at least for me.

But then, sometimes, I'd think how sweet he could be—how sweet we could be together. Tangled up in bed, riding somewhere in the car, or just, on some ordinary day, putting up the screens in springtime, bringing in the wood. And couldn't we go through life, somehow, like that? Wasn't there some other way to be married—different than the ways we'd been married before—some way that worked?

Because we did have, didn't we, that private little world that we'd created. That wordless world that had to do with sex but wasn't just the sex—was what came after, when we were lying deep inside the winter covers, warm and all mixed up with one another. When we at last could sleep.

But then the rest of it. The mornings when we'd already seen each other sleeping with our mouths open and something sticky trickling down the side of our lips and drying there on the side of our chins, a cracked paste. I having poked him in the night to stop his snoring. He lying on his back with his mouth open like a great fish and that deep loud railroad car of a snore coming out of him. And how would it be in the morning to have to look at him with his baggy eyes and his creasy face and his old blue pajamas with a stain on the pants where, during the night, in his hasty midnight trek to the bathroom, he'd inadvertently let some of the urine dribble through? And what about the ways in which I myself would be revealed? My own baggy creasy pocky face in the morning. My own hair standing on end in messy disarray. My own sad slippers. My own secret trips to the bathroom now public knowledge. The smells of each one of us. The hairs in the bathtub curly and tiny and telltale, revealing all.

No. No. I would rather, I often thought, lose him altogether and go on alone than live with him. How we would murder each other finally—not out of passion but out of impatience!

Annoyance. Both of us wanting the phone, the desk, the bathroom, the kitchen, the bed. Both of us wanting our own place but bound together, swaddled in one house sharing and sharing and sharing and bickering needlessly over things that would not even exist if we had our own places to go to and to be alone and to then, as we did then, miss one another in a sweet, sentimental, impossible way.

This was much better, what we had. This is what could work for us, I thought. But he never thought so. Worried about his old age alone. Worried about being left. He worried and felt lonely in the night while I was out with my girlfriends at the movies. While I was chatting on the phone, lying on my couch with a little fire in the fireplace; the snap and sparkle of my pleasant, private dream. Or just happily reading my book and feeling content the way a cat might feel content sitting alone: the warm fire, the snows or the rains outside or the slow sunsets of springtime, the long quiet evenings of summer. All of it darling and dear to me. All of it permanent and happy. All of it cozy and warm. I didn't want him and I didn't need him—at least not all the time. I just wanted him when I wanted him. And then only sometimes.

And that wasn't enough.

"What will become of us?" I asked him now, standing there in the bright woods. The beautiful trees all around and the pleasant air of September. The wonderful sharp smell of the forest in autumn. The bright green moss. The black bark. The pine needles on the path. The clean air of early fall.

"I don't know, Virginia. I don't know," he told me. "I don't know. We'll just go along, I guess."

"Do you think you ought to see a doctor?" I asked him, trying to bring it back around to what started all this. Because without sex, what good was love?

He gave me a look which was an angry look and there was something else, something I didn't recognize, behind that anger.

Later, of course, I knew what it was, but at the time I thought he might be embarrassed by how it was between us. Feeling old because of it. Feeling sad because of it. His failing, falling, faltering testosterone. His coming age. I didn't want to embarrass him further. I didn't want to be demanding, unkind, if he couldn't help it. But later, when I realized what had been really going on, I wished I'd said more—had it out with him right then. But later, of course, it was too late.

Now he stared at me in that unseeing way, then he turned and started off up the path away from me. Said something over his shoulder. "Yeah, I'll talk to the doctor."

But he said it as if I were the naggy mother and he the put-upon adolescent boy—not like he was the man and I was the woman and we were in love.

It did get better after that, didn't it? Not really. I remember the long sad months of that fall when I got busier and busier to compensate for my loneliness. Loneliness of the body. Loneliness of the spirit. Loneliness of the skin. And he complained, when he did complain, that he was lonely, too. But neither of us did anything about it. It was as if we were stuck in the ruts of our decided relationship. He lived in his house and resented me. I lived in my house, both longing for him and dreading his calls. We came together once or twice a week for a movie, for dinner. Still dating after all these years. It didn't really work, but it worked well enough. It was better than nothing. It was better, I thought, much better, than being alone. That part of my life was taken care of. I had someone. After years of hopping from boyfriend to boyfriend, from man to man, leaving as soon as the first, exciting few years wore off and we got to the trudge of it—now, finally I was in an adult relationship. I was an adult. If I was a little bored, this was how it was. How it was for everyone, probably, some of the time. And I could get on with things. Other things. I could stop searching for love because I had it. And sometimes, still, we did have lovely times, didn't we? It worked well enough. It was a journey, I told myself, and there were times when it was bound to be better than other times. I tried to keep hold of this certainty, but sometimes I felt as if I didn't know where we were going, on this muddlesome journey of ours.

Where's he going? I feel the truck make a big turn—right—and the road gets bumpy. I jounce in my waddy nest, glad that it's padded with his old sweaters, the jacket. The bag from Rogerson's, that rests on my ribs, bouncing lightly with each jolt of the Jeep.

I pull the wooly sweater away from my face so I can get

some fresh air, turn my head, and stare up at the roof of the truck. He has no idea I'm here, and I don't know where he's going.

And then I do know. He's driving down the river road, the old road back beside the river. Someday this will get fixed up, too, like the rest of Sinclair, but now it's quiet, junky, and almost abandoned, curving alongside the river and with some sloped dirt turnoffs where teenagers go to smoke pot and get laid on long spring afternoons. We used to come here, too, when we were first going together.

He'd pick me up at work at noon, and we'd get some sandwiches at Judson's and come down here. There's a break in the trees and a clearing with a couple of beat-up picnic tables and a trash can with a crooked lid. We used to watch the river, eat our sandwiches, and talk—back when we had so much to say to one another; still all our stories to tell. Or sometimes we'd just stay in the truck, and not say much, staring out, the radio on or not on, the river going by.

One time, early in our relationship, I put my hand on the back of his neck and held it there. He didn't move. Said nothing. I could feel the prickly hair there, and the rough skin under my hand. It was not young skin, and it reassured me—both the age of his skin, which made him seem permanent and wise, and the way I didn't mind the age of his skin, as if now, finally, I were a mature adult woman in love with a mature adult man and in a new phase of my life—not a girl who went after boys because they were cute or sexy—but that our love was somehow elemental and deep and strong and real and true.

He didn't move. Said nothing.

"Do you mind that?" I asked him. "Me touching you?"

"I like it," he told me. "It used to bother me when women touched me—I mean like that, in the car or something. When I was driving. When I was doing something else. But I like it when you touch me."

I felt as if we had discovered new people in one another, and new people in ourselves through one another. That I was a person I had never been before when I was with him. And he was someone he had never known that he could be. That we'd unlocked something that had been hidden away for years—for years!—but still was fragrant. Amazingly fragrant. Still smelled so sweet.

Now he pulls into what I'm sure is that same dirt and gravel parking area, and though I am hidden down below, behind him, I know exactly what he's seeing: the one big tree with the roots exposed, the shore eroded by all the water that's always rushing by. The late-September leaves are large and full, just starting to turn color. In another week or two they'll fall. This is the last fullness, this is the end of it—the summer. Past summer, really. The chilly first start of the fall.

He turns the engine off and settles back. I can feel the changed pressure of the seat in front of me as he shifts his weight and pushes back against me. Does he really have no idea that I'm here?

This is the moment, certainly, when I should say some-thing.

What would happen if I came out of hiding now? If I finally came out and I talked to him? Just talked to him. Maybe he would be glad to see me. Maybe he would be thrilled to see me. He used to be thrilled. *I adore you,* he'd tell me. *You're it.* I got so used to hearing it, that I began to think it was an ordinary hat—that crown I wore—his love.

Maybe, if I came out now, all this separation and loneliness and longing and anger and sadness would just fly away down the river—and we would be the people that we used to be to-gether, or that I thought we were. All misunderstandings for-gotten. All resentments. All disappointments. We would be the way we had been before, sitting here together under the heavy leaves of late summer, watching the river go by.

Maybe I would climb into the seat beside him—after he got over the initial shock and his heart stopped pounding—and we would hold hands. That's all. Just hold hands. No radio. No words. No conversation. No recriminations and no kisses, even. It would be simple. As simple as water and the ending day.

This is the time when I should speak to him. But I am so tired, down here swaddled in his old sweaters, deep in the dark, musty hiding place where I have burrowed in. And the effort of pushing aside all of this weighty fabric seems impossible. And the explanations and the apology and the embarrassment—too much to overcome. And what if he's angry with me? Or disgusted by me? Or bored by me? Or just sort of surprised and bemused. *What are you doing here?*

Maybe he hasn't been thinking about me the way I've been thinking about him, day after day since the breakup. And then, how would that be? What little shreds of dignity I still have left—*pfft*—would all be gone.

5

No, better to stay down here, deep down and hidden. Let him look at the river all he wants to.

Let him start the truck, as he starts the truck again. Let him back out, turn around, drive off, without knowing I'm here. Let him think he's alone.

I can hear Alan Jackson singing *pop a top for me.* David's window is still open, and cold air floods into the Jeep as he accelerates on what must be the main road. If I were sitting up there with him, in the old days, I would have shivered and said, "It's cold," in a pitiful voice and he would have rolled his window up. "Sorry," he would have said, and he might, if he'd been in the right kind of mood, reached over and put his hand on my knee and held it there and I would have felt so safe! So safe and so happy, to have his hand there on my knee. His big man's hand. Big enough to cup the whole cap, like a father.

You're the one for me. You're it, David used to tell me after we'd made love. *You're the one I've always wanted. What were we doing all those years away from one another?* he would ask.

And I would wonder why I didn't feel that way—not all the way, the way he seemed to. Why there was this cold little stone inside of me. Why there was some part of myself I couldn't give to him.

We're driving so far now. Is he going to Bangor? But there's no point thinking about it. Where we're going. How I'm going to get out of here. How I'm going to get back to my car, parked in the parking lot at Rogerson's Emporium, there by the river. I will. I'll get out of this fix the way I've gotten out of plenty of stuff in the past. Lots of odd scrapes.

You're always getting into something, aren't you? My mother, when I was six, looking down at me with amused exasperation. Hiding in the bushes along the side of the house with chocolate all over my face.

An old friend arrived out of the past. I got his call on a fall day after I'd been going out with David for a few years.

"Dexter?" I knew his voice right away. He wasn't a boyfriend, but we were close. That's what I told David. "We were close," I told him. "We went on trips together."

"Trips? You mean like LSD?" He was old enough never to have done acid, and he didn't quite get it. Didn't like to hear about that part of my life.

But now I pretended that he didn't feel that way. I laughed instead. "Yeah—some of that. But you know. Trips! You know, when you're in college and you just decide let's go to Mexico or New Orleans or something and you pile into a car and you start driving and you pool your money and drive all night and wake up sleeping in the car by the side of the road realizing it's ridiculous and you've got to go back, or thinking it's the greatest, most poetic thing and winding up catching some hideous crabs or something in some rundown cheesy hotel with mice in the walls and a dirty shower?"

He just looked at me. "We've led such different lives," was all he said.

That used to be, I thought, what he found charming.

Dexter turned up that autumn afternoon with a friend he rowed with.

"Rowed?" I asked him.

"Yeah," he said. He was in good shape. He looked the same as he had in college, only more muscular. Going through a divorce. Looking up old girlfriends. He'd gotten more confident. He was shy with me back then, but he wasn't anymore. Now he looked me up and down when we stopped by the big rock on our walk.

"So this is your life," he said, looking at me. "Not quite how I'd imagine you winding up."

I looked back at him.

"So?"

He put his hands in his pockets just the way he used to, shrugged his shoulders.

"So—I don't know. An ad agency? But you look good. You look great, in fact."

He continued looking at me.

"Do you love this guy?"

David had been at the house when Dexter arrived. Just leaving. He'd been down overnight and was going back home, the long bumpy road over the hills. He'd had on a sweater I'd never particularly liked. He'd looked okay, but not quite the way I wanted him to look, when Dexter met him. His recent bad hair-cut. His ugly sweater. But couldn't Dexter see how tall and kind he was?

"Well? Do you?"

I realized that I hadn't answered him.

"I don't know, Dexter," I said, finally. "I like having a boy-friend. He's dear to me. I just don't know if I can love anybody anymore."

Dexter laughed the way I remembered him laughing—a short, hard bark of a laugh. "What do you mean?" he asked, like I was kidding, but I wasn't kidding.

"We have our own two lives. I want that."

"Maybe it's him," Dexter said. "Maybe you don't love him."

"Oh, of course I love him. He's very good to me. But I don't want to marry him, if that's what you mean. If that's how you tell if it's real. I don't want to live with him. I want to keep sepa-rate."

"Why's that?"

"I guess partly because getting divorced was so hard. I never want to go through that again. How sad it was. How lonely I felt after. Or maybe I'm just selfish. I like being on my own. I want someone in my life, but not necessarily in my home. I don't want to talk to them all the time; to account for myself. My kids and I have our own little systems and rituals. I don't want to mess that up, and I don't want the dreariness of marriage and the inevitability of it. And, mostly, I think, I don't want to feel bad when it's over."

"You're kidding yourself. You would anyway, wouldn't you? You've been going together for a while now, haven't you? For what? Three? Four years?" Dexter asked me.

"Yeah. But we don't live together. We're not entwined. I could peel him away out of my life at any time and it wouldn't leave a scar."

I really believed that by keeping some part of myself away from David—by not living with him, by not marrying him, I could protect myself. And now that he's gone I don't know what I think anymore. About what I did; what maybe I should have done.

And I don't know now, jouncing along in the back of his Jeep, don't know if I love him and miss him and am sad that he left me, or if I'm out for vengeance. Maybe both.

I know that since the end of our relationship, I've felt un-hooked. Back out in the world in a way that is familiar and not familiar. It feels odd, after all those years of being with somebody, to be alone again. There are so many parts to it, the oddness of how it feels. There's the part that's easy to describe—missing him. Missing the contact, the touching, the arm around me, the hand to hold. All of that. The physical part of having a boyfriend. I keep forgetting he's not there. Sleep feels, as it of-ten has felt at hard times in my life, as precious as money. Like a dear escape from my sadness. I long for it. I plan around it. I make sure I get enough exercise every day. It feels like another sort of chore—tiring myself enough to sleep.

Not having someone after having someone so long. It's an empty feeling—the abyss is closer—my own mortality is nearer than it was. At first it felt, in those first few weeks, like a crude amputation. I kept picturing it like that: a horrible wrenching and chop. The pain so enormous that I couldn't even feel it at first. I spent the first morning just reeling, spent the first month in a daze. But gradually it settled into a dull, painful ache. And I would think—*Oh, okay, so this is how it is, I have to live with this dull pain for awhile, and then, gradually, it will get better.* Like the time I had that operation and it hurt for a long time and then just a twinge now and then, and then, gone.

Only it's not as easy as that—losing a person. You lose so many parts of him in so many different and unexpected places. It reminds me of how it felt when I quit smoking. I'd been smoking and smoking away, and then, after ten years, I suddenly quit—just like that. One day I was smoking a pack and a half and the next day I wasn't smoking at all. I felt terrible, sad, and exhausted—and then there were the unexpected ways it haunted me. Everywhere I turned I was not smoking. Not smoking in the car when I was driving. Not smoking after making love. Not smoking with my coffee at the drugstore counter. Not smoking when I sat at my desk. Not smoking on the sunny porch late in the afternoon. Not smoking after eating. Not smoking first thing in the morning. Not smoking when I had a drink at night.

And now I was not seeing David. Not calling David anymore. Not having David in my life. Not seeing David on Saturday nights—not having supper with him at Donegal's or Front Street, not going to the movies at the old Century Theatre with its bunchy old red velvet chairs. Not spending Sunday mornings with David—not having brunch at Dog Tree, not walking in the sunny woods, not sitting on my porch in the afternoon reading *The New York Times.*

And I didn't know how to be without him. Couldn't figure out how it felt because it felt so odd. He'd just been there. A fact of my life. And now he wasn't there anymore and there was nothing else to replace him. Everything else: the rooms of my house, the path in the woods, the nights and the weekends were the same, but without him everything was completely different.

I felt disconnected. I had this image in my mind in which I had tentacles coming out of me that had reached out all arosund me, writhing in the air, seeking a place to attach themselves to. When I tried to explain it to my friend Susan it sounded vaguely disgusting—like some sort of icky science fiction movie you wish you hadn't seen, knowing it will invade your dreams with its tentacular horrors. I couldn't explain it, but I had a clear interior picture of what it felt like—those winding graspy arm things coming off of me, looking for a place to fasten onto, waving, useless—blind, headless snakes in the lonely air.

I had been attached to David. He'd been my other self. A bad self, sometimes. A self I was scornful of, cruel to maybe, dismissive of sometimes, but part of me. And was I really so bad?

...

I remember when we were first getting to know one another—two broken, divorced people long single, me with my two kids and my managerial position at the ad agency, making waffles on Sunday morning, dressing up in severe suits for meetings in the boardroom. A mixed life. Sometimes I wasn't sure which one I was—the cozy mommy reading stories or the tight-lipped businesswoman in my office. Very busy I felt in those days. Very important. And lonely, too, with nowhere to lie down.

And then David came along and everything switched over. I felt young again. I *was* young. I was only forty. I had felt so old. Now, suddenly, I was young beneath his touch. My skin felt lustrous, unbelievable. My body felt like a new body, not just something to be washed and dressed and exercised and endured, but something wonderful and precious—my own skin! I was as proud of it as I had been proud of it when I was sixteen, seventeen, and had my breasts and my hips to display in my tight hip-hugger blue jeans. I'd been amazed by myself back then, and now I got to be amazed by myself all over again.

How he made me feel. Sitting in a restaurant together, looking across the table, smiling at one another. I felt perfect.

Riding in his truck—I had looked over, seen the side of his face, and he turned and gave me a wolfish grin that frightened and thrilled me. Thrilled me.

I adore you, he would tell me, pressing his body against my body in the tangled sheets. The children gone off to their father's, my house like a borrowed house, the rooms changed by the children's absence so that, for one night, one weekend, it was only ours.

I hadn't thought I'd get this again—this kind of love, this swoopiness and giddiness and loveliness I felt when I was with him. I had thought, during my marriage, after my marriage, that I was doomed to dry years now. I had felt old and competent and used up. I had felt sensible and tidy and passed over.

But now, with David, everything was different. And I thought from the start that if we didn't get married, if we never lived together, if we didn't allow ourselves to become ordinary, to grind away at each other the way people grind away at each other when they are together too much, too long, enduring the sad same plow of events, the terrible ordinary tribulations of life—that we could remain romantic and perfect and just like this forever.

But of course not.

Even without the marriage, even without living together, life can flatten, become predictable. You can fall into patterns. Maybe the thing to do—I thought later—is to just jump on the bus when you first fall in love with someone. Just jump fearlessly aboard in that first flush of promise, that terrible rapture. Get married right away or move in together—then figure it out. But I was reluctant—we both were, I think. My children were young and we had formed, in our years as a family of three, a tight little unit. I didn't want to jar that or jostle what felt like a stable family. I thought we could wait.

How could I manage a marriage and still manage all of my

life? My children needed me. Their lives were so busy. And then, when my dad got sick, it was all I could do to hold it together for them, for my mother, for all of us.

That was a hard time, but I got through it. I went to work.

Work somehow was the safest thing. Work didn't tear at my heart. Work had a beginning and an end. Work was what defined me. Work gave me money, which I needed so I could pay for all the things my children needed. Work and money. Money and work. These were the things of my life. Work made me feel competent when all of the world was conspiring to make me feel incompetent, helpless, broken, lost. If I could just go to work I would be all right, or so I thought.

So I worked. And when I didn't work, and I wasn't at the hospital, or at my parents' house, I was exhausted. I lay on the couch. David came over and he wanted to talk to me. Something with his big business deal I had begun not to believe in, though I still turned to him wearily. *Sure. I'm sure it'll work out. You'll see.*

I thought he understood that I was doing what I had to do— taking care of my children. Helping my mother cope with my dad's illness, helping my dad get well. And David seemed to be okay—or mostly okay, but maybe I was just too busy to notice. I was so busy. He was just there. Then, when I turned back to look at him—he was different. He was sad, he'd moved away from me. So was it all my fault? Partly my fault? Entirely my fault? Was he just the kind, befuddled man trying to do the right thing, riding the wild waves of my life with me, stretching out his hand to me, propping me up on my tiny skiff as I bounced and heaved? Was it all me? Was it all my fault? When I saw how sad he'd become, when he got so quiet, shouldn't I have taken him more seriously? Shouldn't I have done something?

And things did get better for a while, didn't they? He did seem much better. And all that was years ago, wasn't it? What was wrong now?

You need to see someone, I kept telling him last fall. Maybe you need to go on medication for a while. He would never do that, he told me, never. He wasn't going to take drugs. I said, *Maybe you should talk to somebody,* but then he would say there was nobody good to talk to and besides, he had me. And then I felt as if I were lying on the bed in my parents' bedroom when they had big loud parties downstairs, when all the ladies wore fur coats. My sister and I would stroke the coats and roll around on them and pull them over ourselves and rub our faces on the fur. It was so soft. And my sister would be the one to get up first and say, *We're going to get in trouble, better get off them, Virginia,* but I would want to stay just one more minute with my face against the softness of the fur. My sister would go out of the room in her pajamas and then right away come back in again out of the dark hallway into the soft glow of our parents' bedroom which was lit with a single lamp with a white cloth shade. *Come on!* my sister would say again, and finally I would come away.

I would have liked to have stayed there always, lying on that bed heaped high with coats. But when I was with David in that last, sad year, I felt as if I were back there again, lying on that bed, but this time with all of the coats on top of me and pressing down, their great, dark, heavy weight, huge, heavy pelts, the fur now foreign, slightly greasy to the touch, unclean. That's how it felt—the burden of his love and his depression.

One afternoon it smelled funny in the Jeep and I remarked on it. "Smells kind of like pretzels," I said.

He made a sour face. Lately he had forgotten all his lines. All of his usual retorts to my usual remarks. Stuff we had said and said again and again over the years, building up, as couples do, a little recognizable refrain of remarks and retorts, questions and answers, quips and snips of words. It was all familiar and dear to me. I thought it was also dear to him.

Again, I asked about medication, and again he refused.

"I don't want medication," he said stubbornly.

"I know. I wouldn't want it, either," I said. I did understand that. I did disdain this growing trend of everybody taking everything; trying to fix their problems with a pill. I thought people ought to just get more exercise. Ought to buck up. Ought to change their life around if it didn't suit them. Ought to get over it with their mothers, already. Ought to quit their lousy jobs and get another job—a job they liked. Divorce their shabby husbands or their naggy wives. Ought to go out and do something. That's what I did. But I hadn't ever really suffered from depression. Hadn't ever really gotten to that place, that gray place where, my friend Marie explained, you could wander for years.

"What was it like?" I asked her once, when she was better.

"It's like you're wading through something deep and heavy. It's like everything is an enormous effort. Like nothing gives you any pleasure. That nothing will ever change. You feel as if it's all your fault, too. You can't stop circling inward."

Was that what David was feeling now? Wading through something deep and heavy? And why couldn't I be kinder about it? Why couldn't I say the one thing that would change all that? The one thing that would make him feel better? Why didn't I know what it was?

I tried to get him to talk to me. But it was the same, always the same, when he tried to explain how he felt. But maybe, I thought later, he couldn't explain it because he wasn't telling the truth.

The worst part was that it didn't seem as if it was ever going to change.

"Don't you think you ought to do something?" I'd ask him. "Don't you think you ought to see someone?"

I got the name of a psychologist.

He had the name for weeks before he did anything about it. Then, finally, he made an appointment, announcing it to me importantly, as if he'd just clinched a huge deal.

"Well, I made an appointment with that guy," he said over the phone one day.

"Great!" I said. "When do you see him?"

"In a couple of weeks," he told me, and I was dismayed. I didn't think I could take a couple of weeks more of this. I wasn't sure he could.

"Let's get away," I suggested, and we went to Canada for the weekend; to an old inn high on a rocky bluff over the sea, the tidy village far below; green grassy park. Because it was fall—last fall—already, we were able to get the room we liked with three broad windows and a view of the sea. Maybe this would be the weekend we remembered as the beginning of the better time.

We walked down into the village, the way we always had, but he was leaden beside me, silent and furrowed with thought. We sat on the long veranda in the evening, after supper in the book-lined library with our brandy, rode bikes along the wide road that led past the golf courses and along the shore—but it wasn't the same.

In other years we had both been delighted with the faux formal old-fashioned charm of the place. The wonderful bacon at breakfast, the quiet bench in the seaside park, the smell of yarn in the shop, but now I had to do it all alone—display that pleasure. I felt like a gibbering monkey—a naggy child, tugging at her parent's balky hand—*come on come on!* It was dreadful.

Being with David that fall was like dragging a sack of rocks around the room.

"Let's go to that garden we went to last year."

"It's past the season. There won't be much left in it."

"Well, let's go look."

"If you want to, I guess."

In bed—always in bed—which I knew was the wrong place, I asked him again, "Are you okay?"

He lay beside me. Heavy. So heavy and still. His head propped up on the folded pillow.

"I don't know, Virginia," he said. "Sometimes I just want to drive off the road. I sit at my desk and I can't do anything. I can't concentrate to work."

"You really have to see somebody."

"Yeah," he said.

I put my arms around him. His skin felt damp, almost chilly.

"Are you cold?" I asked him.

"No," he said. "I just want to go to sleep," he told me.

How could I have thought that was normal?

6

I have been lulled into thinking I will be here forever. The motion of the truck is so soothing, and I am sleepy here under the pile of sweaters and jackets and the brown paper shopping bag he tossed in on top of me, which at first was sort of digging into my side, but now feels comfortable, right. I am used to the smell back here—old pretzels, rain slicker, wool. Up front I can hear him still tunelessly humming along with some imagined, invisible music. The window is open and the breeze is chilly but not unpleasant. I feel almost good.

I have no idea where we are or where he is going, when he will stop or what he will do when he gets wherever he's headed. I'm relaxed, but I've begun wondering, again, almost idly, as if I were watching a comfortable, slightly boring movie, what comes next. What am I supposed to do? What if, when he stops driving, he starts rooting around back here looking for something and discovers me? How can I gracefully get out of this one? I have wanted our next meeting—when we finally did see each other again after nine months, ten months, to be triumphant—for me.

It would be better if I were the one to surprise him. So should I just go ahead and rear up now? Or speak from my depths, in a sepulcher voice, speak his name? But what if I rear up and he's so startled he goes off the road? And then I might also be injured. And if I do speak—wouldn't that freak him out also? Or would he even hear me over the sound of the engine and the sound of his own solitary, breathy humming? What if I finally get my courage up and say something and then he doesn't hear me and so I have to say it again, and he still doesn't hear me and so I say it again, louder this time, and then again, louder still, and he *still* doesn't hear me until finally I'm shouting—shouting his name? And what would I say, anyway? *Hi?* Or *Hello*—does that have more dignity?

But I don't have to decide anything, after all. The truck turns suddenly. I'm jostled about in back. And he stops.

November: a cold, surly day. Black tree branches sharp against gray sky, the cold harsh wind.

I had a meeting in the afternoon. It was supposed to snow later on. On the way into Sinclair I noticed that *Something's Gotta Give* was playing at the shopping center. We could go to the six o'clock, maybe, if I caught him.

I tried David from the pay phone downtown, standing outside on the sidewalk on the steep hill leading down to Rogerson's on the other side of the bridge.

The same place I had stood, same phone I'd used, the year before, when I was on my way to Sinclair and heard the news of the Twin Towers on the radio. Stunned, I had driven into town, parked the car, used the pay phone to call David.

I had stood there with the cold phone pressed to my ear. The sky unbelievably blue. Downtown Sinclair the same as ever: brick buildings, wooden buckets of red geraniums along the sidewalks, green-striped awnings on the shops, the old-fashioned movie theater, the health food store.

"David?"

"Yeah!" he'd said, as if it were an emergency.

"What's going on?"

"I'm watching it right now on TV," he'd told me. "Oh God, there it goes! The building just came down."

"The whole building?"

"Yes."

"Are we at war?"

"I don't know."

"What should I do?"

"Where are you?"

"Sinclair. Main Street."

"You're probably okay. I guess just go ahead and do whatever you're doing."

"Are we at war?" I asked him again.

"I don't know, Virginia. I don't know."

There was a little pause. I looked at the blue sky some more. It seemed so tranquil, that bright blue September sky over the town of Sinclair. But, knowing what I knew, the blue seemed ominous. It was as if I could see it there—bombs exploding, buildings crashing apart, great walls of flames. Nothing would ever be the same anymore, I thought. We'll never be safe again.

"I'm scared," I told him.

"It'll be all right," he said. "Look, why don't you come down here?"

And so, instead of going to work, I had driven to his house and he had been there at the door when I arrived, waiting for me with his hair standing on end and his old green sweater and his reassuring hug against his strong warm chest and we had gone into the study and watched it all—the wreckage, the terror, the endless, silent, screaming faces of the crowd.

Now, in November, a year later, the year he was always depressed, I held the same phone to my ear and dialed his number. It was cold out. It was going to snow. The first snow of winter. There was no answer until the machine picked up. I left a message, saying I'd call back later. "Maybe we could go to the movie. Wouldn't that be nice?" I'd take him to dinner, after, if he wanted. We could go to Donegal's. We hadn't been there in a while.

When I hung up I felt happy, almost gay, having heard his voice, even his answering machine voice. Maybe he was feeling better now. Maybe we could have a wonderful night together. Maybe I'd wind up staying at his house and it would be snowing and we'd have to stay inside and make do with whatever he had for breakfast in the morning—with all that snow outside. The first real snow of the season. How it seemed, each year, so wonderful, so dear.

I called him back a little later, using a phone at the bank, and again, from April's, where I bought some lacy underwear I thought he'd like.

Just in case, I thought. If I do go down and spend the night.

But he wasn't there again when I called. So I called his cell phone and his home phone.

It was five o'clock, but we could still make the movie if he hurried. I called him again, this time from the movie theater at the shopping center. Outside in the parking lot I could see the snow beginning to fall: small tiny flakes, the kind that keep on coming. The sky was dark and it looked like the storm would last.

This time he was there.

"Did you get my messages?"

"I just got in," he told me.

"I called about ten times! I called your cell phone and I called your house. Where were you?"

"I was at the office."

"Oh! I thought you were just out somewhere. I should have called down there. I didn't think you'd be there on a Saturday."

"Yeah," he said. "I was."

"So what do you think?" I asked him. I was tired now, but finally getting him, just hearing his voice, made me feel better. "Want to go to the movies?"

"It's snowing," he told me.

I glanced out through the wide windows at the parking lot, at the snow, like bits of litter, sprinkling down from the sky. "Not so much," I told him. "Just a little."

"It's supposed to get really bad," he said.

He sounded funny. Angry, almost. He got so worried when I drove in snow. Probably that was it.

"Are you okay?"

His voice was like the voice of someone who is doing something else, who is reading a paper while they're talking with you, or looking for something under the desk.

"Yeah, I'm fine. I think you ought to go home. It's supposed to snow a lot. Six to ten inches."

"Oh," I said, like a kid, I remembered later. Later I thought how I had sounded: plaintive, childish, utterly in the dark. Stupid. She was probably right there—Natalie—the woman he was seeing—the one I didn't know about or even suspect. She was probably right there with him listening in, or right in the other room, or maybe upstairs in the bathroom, and he had come down to the kitchen to make his call. The red light on the answering machine flashing impatiently. Four calls, all mine, recorded in various stages of stupid enthusiasm. He might have been in bed with Natalie while I walked up and down Main Street in the cold November air. Back and forth. Rogerson's. April's, waiting to reach him. Maybe he had forgotten to turn down the sound on the answering machine. Maybe they had been making love when my first call came. The sound of the phone. Both of them frozen, guilty, in the covers.

"I don't have to get it," he tells her, pulling her toward him—her alien fish body, her strange, alien face.

The phone keeps ringing. He's kissing her. Finally the answering machine kicks in downstairs and they hear his voice saying his name, saying his phone number, asking the caller to please leave a message after the tone. Then my voice. Too loud, too childish, somewhat nasal over the answering machine. I never sound like myself on machines. I sound like some other woman. Some stupid woman in an ugly coat.

"David? Listen! I'm in Sinclair. Guess what's playing at the Mall?"

He looks at her ruefully. "I'm sorry," he tells her. "I know this is awkward for you."

But I thought all this later, of course. Long after the phone message had been erased. Long after the snow had melted and new snow had fallen, and we were through with all that—the explanations and the realizations. After I had gone over and over each moment I could remember from the last few months. Each moment, each time we spoke, each time something happened and I'd thought, like Miss Clavel, Something is not right.

I had thought, even then, that it was kind of odd that he didn't invite me down to his house that night.

Odd, I thought, the other time I was trying to reach him and he didn't call for hours.

Odd, when he was going on that sailing trip back in September and I suggested that I meet him down the coast and he said he wasn't sure exactly where he was going, that he didn't want to plan, that it would be too hard to arrange to meet me. We'd done that before and it had been nice. But this time, no.

Odd.

I thought he was acting so odd.

•••

And that other time, when I asked again. We were at my house, in the bed. He was lying there on his back with his eyes shut. We had tried again to make love but—nothing. His penis, when I touched it, felt wilted, cool.

I was lying against him, my breast against his upper arm. My skin felt hot. I pushed up against him. That used to be all it took, but not now.

"What's the matter?"

"I don't know," he told me. He opened his eyes, stared straight up at the ceiling. "I don't know."

Was he just old? Was it that prostate business? The hidden gland that was supposed to be a certain size, the size of a walnut. Had that gland swollen to immense proportions? The size of a coconut, maybe? He didn't like to talk about it.

"Do you think you ought to see the doctor again?"

I was near him, looking at the side of his face, which was dear to me and familiar. His hair all messy from lying on the bed, the line of his jaw. When he spoke to me it was like a slap.

"Will you just leave me alone?"

I rolled away, and then what? Then I said, "I'm sorry."

Later on, after all the rest of it, that was what haunted me. How I had apologized, how I had worried about things I had said to provoke him, to irritate him, to hurt him, to criticize him. If only, I'd thought, I could be kinder, sweeter, more understanding, younger, prettier, thinner—then none of this would be happening.

It was as if each of us were doing our own private dance—

full of interior explanations for one another's behavior—a continuous conversation that we never said out loud.

When he was married, he'd told me, and he and Joan weren't getting along, he used to drive his car down to the shore after work and just sit there in his car, watching the wind on the water, watching the waves come in. He didn't want to go home. He would just sit there and be sad. And I felt, each time I heard that story, how different things would have been if I'd been there then. If I'd been there to comfort him, to talk to him, to sit beside him in the car, to make him laugh.

I felt sometimes as if it were just the two of us in a cozy little nest—the two of us outside the world together. When we were at a restaurant and made up stories about the people at the other tables. The sad couple reading books while they waited for their dinners to arrive. The furious lesbian couple. The elegant man alone. We talked about our families, our friends, people we knew from work. The two of us were in a secret little club. We understood things the same way. We had our own private language. Secret signs and handshakes. Signals we'd invented in the dark.

I felt sorry for the lonely man in the car sitting at the shore all those years ago, not knowing me. Not knowing us.

Later, I thought—was he telling his new girlfriend, Natalie, about *me*? Saying he was lonely in *our* relationship? Saying that he sat down in his car by the shore? Telling her the things that he used to tell me?

Later, after the breakup, I lay in bed and thought again and again about all those same things—going over and over them obsessively as if somewhere in the shuffle of events and memories there was one card I would find that would make everything make sense. Or maybe I was searching for the one card I could play and change the way things had turned out.

December. The Christmas office party.

"Are you sure you don't mind going?"

Lately it seemed as if everything was a big chore for him. As if he were carrying around a great weight.

"I don't mind."

"Okay, well, why don't we meet at the Dreamwood Pines? We can meet in the lobby."

"Okay."

And didn't he sound a little better? I thought so. Just two days before, I had come home to find my house full of flowers. He had bought dozens of flowers and stuck them in vases all over my house, with a note on the kitchen table in great big letters: *Virginia, I love you. David.*

What was he trying to tell me? *Thank you for hanging in? I know I've been acting weird, but I'm through with that now? Don't worry, I'll come back to you?*

"I'll come back to you," he whispered, lying in bed beside me. "Just hold on, and I'll find my way back."

I wait in the Christmassy lobby. I'm all dressed up for the party. Wearing my pretty green velvet pants and my black cashmere sweater, these really pointy party shoes that look terrific. I can't stand very long in them, or walk anywhere, but that's part of their charm. The sparkly necklace David gave me once that I wear at holiday time.

There's a little fake Christmas tree in the hotel lobby full of red shiny balls and silver shiny balls and tiny white lights. I sit on the maroon couch and look at the presents under the tree.

Other members of the agency come in with their coats on, bright-cheeked from the cold, say *Hi!* to me and pass by into the rooms beyond where the party has already started. Every time the doors to the back room swing open I can hear the music, then the door flips shut again and I can hear only the sound of the street outside, cars going past.

"Hey!" Scott Wilkinson, an account exec, comes out from the party. "What are you doing out here? You get stood up?"

David arrives. He's got on his good coat. His hat. The one I bought him. But he looks wrong.

"Are you okay?"

His face is grayish, wrong-colored, though he just came in from the cold. He has his nervous expression on, stands there before me in his coat. He looks older, thinner. His head looks smaller, and the hat too large.

"Are you okay?"

"I don't feel so good," he tells me. He doesn't even glance at Scott, who mumbles something about *see you inside* and fades back into the party.

"What's the matter?"

I stand up, and right away my shoes start hurting. I want to grab them off and stump around in my socks, but I can't do that.

I get close to him. His breath is terrible. His face really doesn't look right, and he won't meet my gaze. His eyes keep darting away. Little pale blue eyes, darting around, looking at me and darting away again.

"I don't know. It's my stomach," he tells me. "It's really up-set."

"Oh, you shouldn't have come!" I say. "Do you want to go home?"

"No, I'll be okay," but he doesn't look right and I wish he would just go home and later I wish he *had* gone home, because he won't eat anything, won't talk to anyone, just sits down in a chair and stares moodily before him, sipping a ginger ale, saying, "No, I don't think I should have anything to drink," in a mournful way.

Later, when I'm talking with someone, one of the guys I work with, David comes over, stands near me, lurking around, then touches my arm.

I turn toward him and he's close to me and he smells funny. Like a sick person. Like a sick person who's been drinking ginger ale and who might throw up.

"I'm getting chills," he tells me. "Is it really cold in here?"

It's actually kind of hot, and my feet are killing me.

"No. Maybe you should go home," I tell him again. "Do you want me to drive you?"

"No! I'm okay," he says. "I'm just cold."

Then he goes back to his chair. One of the ladies from the Bangor office goes over and sits with him, and I see him talking to her. Telling her one of his long stories, I suspect. Then I turn back to the man I was talking with. David must not be too sick; he would have gone home, I think.

Later, of course, that's another scene I replay in my mind. Shouldn't I have bundled him into the car and driven him home? Shouldn't I have been more worried and less annoyed by him? Shouldn't I have left the party, taken him back to his house, to my house, and put him to bed and been nicer? Shouldn't I have been nicer altogether? Always?

I remember each time I spoke sharply to him. Each time I glanced at him and was annoyed to see him licking his lips in his nervous way, darting his eyes around, rubbing his face, falling asleep with his mouth open and a book on his chest. Those things that used to make me feel crazy later seem dear to me— his darling bad habits, his foibles. But I know, if I am honest with myself, that if he were here again, doing those things again, it would still drive me crazy.

The sound of his breathing. The way he would troop off to the bathroom with his big book on the Civil War as if he were setting up shop in there. The way he had to always have seconds of everything, even when he wasn't hungry. Eat way more than he needed, and then complain that he felt too full, he was putting on weight—as if it were my fault.

The way he showed off. The way he insisted on things that he really knew nothing about. His imperious *No! That's not right!* when anyone dared to differ. Talking in a loud voice at restaurants about the ingredients of the dish before him. Consulting the wine steward as if he knew anything about it. Grumbling if the waiter was late with our order; shifting around in his chair, annoyed. Craning around to look at the door to the kitchen. Muttering about sloppy service. Making a dumb joke and then sticking his tongue out like a big wet raw sausage. *Disgusting,* I always thought when he did that. *Disgusting.*

All of those things would still disgust me, enrage me almost, if I were in a certain mood. But then I would probably do that thing I did, would talk myself back into loving him—*Yes, but he is so good to me. Yes, but he is so true. Yes, but he's always there for me.* The dog by the door. The one I can trust. The one man who truly truly loves me. The one that I've got.

"I love you so much," he said to me. "You're the one."

And how could I turn my back on that adoration? How could I discard that kind of devotion? When would I, at forty-five, forty-eight, fifty-one, ever find anyone else who would love me with that strong tide of love—the way that he loved me? No one. Not ever. I knew.

When I replayed the Christmas party scene in my mind I felt guilty and uncomfortable. Why wasn't I more sympathetic that night? Why only annoyed? He was sick. He was shaky and weak. But then I think what came only two weeks later—then the fierce fury, which is much more comfortable than regret, comes back to me. And I am like a woman with a sword. Like a woman with a sword of my anger. Indignant. Virtuous. Victorious and beautiful in my rage.

Of course he was sick! Sick with guilt! He was sick because he'd probably spent the whole afternoon in bed with Natalie. Even thinking the name makes me angry. Gives me a thrill, almost. A chill. *Natalie.* Of course he was sick. He was figuring out how to tell me, *what* he would tell me, *if* he would tell me, *how much* he would tell me. And there he was at my office Christmas party surrounded by people who worked with me, who liked me, who kept coming up to me, grabbing my arm, giving me a hug—*Virginia! Virginia!*—and I smiling and hugging this one and that. And asking about their children and grandchildren in my friendly fucking way and introducing him and looking around for him and he slumped over in his chair looking sour and sick and ashen-faced and I turning my back again.

How he must have loathed me that night! My gay imperviousness to his despair! My blithe assumption that he'd get over it. My uncaring ways! How he must have resented me and been angry with me and sat there sullenly thinking *she doesn't care she doesn't care if I'm sick, if I'm dying here,* but also, probably, with some cruel, cold part of his brain thinking in a taunting way, *I know something she doesn't know. I know something.*

He must have felt as if he had some power, finally, in our relationship. That while I neglected him, was too busy to see him, had other plans or other friends coming over, or gave him an impatient look—while I did all of those things—all that time, he had a secret that would hurt me, when he chose to reveal it. And though he must have told himself that he felt terrible about what he was doing, he probably didn't feel so terrible. He probably felt pretty wonderful. Probably felt kind of proud—what he'd kept all this time: his small, precious, poisonous secret, his Natalie.

I saw him as old, used up, and tiresome—what did I know? He had a new girl who thought he was wonderful. The woman I would later imagine in various incarnations. Little Natalie with her long shiny brown hair. Little Natalie with her pert, young, unsuckled breasts. Little Natalie who was only five foot three; who was graceful, lithe, and six foot one, who had blue eyes and blonde hair; had green eyes and black hair; who wore neat cabled sweaters; who wore vivid handmade shirts from Peru; who had high heels; who always wore sensible shoes; who was smart; who was fun; who was frisky and new. Little Natalie, the one he was seeing when I was not there.

And how he must have enjoyed knowing his secret. Sucking on it like a sore tooth in that private, meditative, pleasurable way. Enjoyed the guilt, the secrecy, the hastily arranged meetings, the cumbersome, tricky explanations that I always accepted. I with my tiresome faith in him! I with my smug self-assurance. He must have realized that I hadn't noticed, and that made him bolder but also it probably made him angry. My not noticing, not even suspecting, somehow made him more indignant. *How dare she not know?* Didn't I even care that he was having an affair? Didn't I have any feelings left for him? I took him for granted. He was right to do this. He almost *had* to.

He told himself I didn't care and he felt aggrieved by my not caring and felt that he was only doing what anyone would do.

I wonder how he must he have felt, when I used to talk about our friends Rick and Peggy—when Peggy had discovered Rick was getting way too close to his leading lady at the Century Theatre? When Rick finally admitted his affair, he had said in his holier-than-thou, grieving voice that he of course loved Peggy but that he had a true spiritual connection to the other woman. To his, what was her name? Monica. That he and Monica were not lovers. That they had something *very special* between them. There was a bond they'd formed backstage. That they were going through the same sorts of things.

And Peggy, angry and defensive, had yelled at him, *Well, fuck you! I'm your wife!* and had marched him off to counseling, where, under the combined relentless pressure of his angry wife and the clever psychologist, he'd cracked and admitted to a two-month affair and had foresworn it and then, finally, admitted that it had actually been going on for a year, but now he'd never, never do anything like that again, and Peggy made him go with her to see Monica and have it out and all of these things she repeated to me in a hissy voice in the soup section of the supermarket.

And, at the end of it, standing by the croutons, I asked her, "But why do you want him back after all that?"

And Peggy looked at me as if startled by the question, and then she said, "He's my husband. I need him in my life."

And she also said, "Look, Virginia, I'm fifty-nine years old—who else am I going to get?"

I repeated all this to David of course, over supper one night at Front Street. I expected him to react more, was surprised at how uninterested he seemed in the story. Usually he liked this kind of gossip. Liked to discuss other people's shenanigans with me. I would have thought he'd be angry at Rick, more sympathetic to Peggy, or have some theory about how and why. But he kept pretty quiet.

Later, after it was all over, after he was gone, I would play and replay our conversations of the past few months—the months when he was seeing Natalie. I would think of how I must have seemed to him, in the light of what else he was thinking about, in the light of everything else he was doing.

How I must have looked to him, taking off my clothes to go to bed. How I must have looked first thing in the morning in my ugly bathrobe with the coffee stain down the front. Things like that. Pictures of myself when I had felt relaxed and cozy, safe. When he must have been watching me, deciding, weighing each stain—should he keep me? Should he tell me now?

I thought over and over again about the things I'd said and the ways I'd acted. And it was all bad. How he must have hated me, as he moved away from me, as he made his judgments and decisions about me without allowing me any defense, without allowing me a chance to explain, to right myself, to behave differently, to seduce him, win him back, to make him see that I was somehow necessary to him, was still adorable, that I could change.

That was all I wanted. To be adorable. To be adored. I would have done anything to win him back, I thought later, when it was too late. I would have done things differently, if I had known.

I trusted him. He was my standard of honesty. He was my solid man. He was the one I asked, *What should I do? Is this right? Would it be right to do that?* Because, for all the rest of it, I believed that finally, absolutely, he was good. That he was a good man. A good, kind man. And all the rest of it was unimportant in the face of that truth, in the fact of his great love.

7

He pulls over, turns off the Jeep, and suddenly, without warning, he reaches over into the back—into my territory, where I am nestled. Fishes around with his hand awhile. I can feel his fingers, just the tips of them. He is looking for something. He makes an impatient noise and then pulls his arm back in. Didn't he know I was there?

He opens the truck door, gets out, and the whole truck lightens.

I hear his footsteps and a clanking sound. He's getting gas. If I were to sit up now, look out the window, I'd be able to see him. I am so tempted. Just to see his face. I can imagine how it would look, turned away from me the way he turns his face away when he is pumping gas. Maybe I would tap on the window and smile at him and he would smile back. Before he had a chance to think about it. Before he remembered that he had another girlfriend. He'd look right at me and then maybe he'd sort of roll his eyes. *Oh, Virginia!* And then—and then, I guess, just finish pumping the gas.

Another clank and he closes the gas tank, shuts the little door, and I hear him walk away across the pavement.

I do move now. I feel stiff. I slowly rise until I'm looking out the window. We're at the gas station that's on the way to his house, a modern approximation of a log cabin. We have often stopped here and bought cold drinks on summer afternoons. Buddy and his wife, Donna, run the place. David's probably talking to one of them now.

Haven't seen that girl you used to go with—what was her name? The one from down the coast? In a while.

Or are they used to seeing Natalie now? And are they asking about her?

I see the door to the gas station open, duck down, and then David's back in the truck, and the music's on again. It's starting to feel normal—as if I belong back here. The kid in the backseat under the sleeping bag. It's almost restful.

At least now I know where we're going. We're headed to his house. We won't just be driving forever. Although in a way, maybe that's what I want. That's what I wanted all along, wasn't it—when we were together? That's why I fought so hard against knowing we no longer loved each other. Against knowing what was really wrong between us. I wanted things to be the same forever—to just drive, like this, with him at the wheel—with me hidden down in the back, driving along with no destination—in a sort of suspended timelessness—just driving along the serene and swoopy asphalt roads of Maine.

And all this time thoughts are going through my head like places you pass on a road—the white house with the bunchy hedge in front, the small convenience store with dark red shingles. Places you know by heart, for having passed them so often. Things that happened a long time ago. Things that happened in the last year. The sad time after the breakup—all those long winter months alone. All alone forever it felt like. When you feel the sharp edge of despair, you feel the entire sword. It felt permanent. I would always be alone. I would always be hanging over the abyss. The rest of my life marching along and me with it, trying to keep up.

What did other people do? I wondered. Losing spouses to divorce, to Alzheimer's, to death? How do they survive after such enormous losses? That sudden, abrupt amputation and then, after that, everything off kilter forever. How do you walk without that arm you're so used to? How do you keep your balance? The sharp pain that feels unending, without dimension, limitless, and then the ache and the ache and the ache that goes on and on; that comes in a wave and recedes and comes back and then comes back again. It was underneath everything—that sadness. Right under all the surface emotions: delight, detail, determination. There it was—the sadness—a big, spongy slab of it.

Why did I still think that happiness was something I could acquire—like a new dress? Why did I think happiness would just come to me if I behaved myself, worked hard, ate right, kept clean, and got enough exercise? Happiness comes when you least expect it, not on order.

Some days I thought maybe I ought to distract myself with love—even a bright and giddy infatuation—but there was nobody else I could even imagine. No one looked good to me. The young ones were too young. I had no interest in them, with their big brown heads of bushy hair and their big, confident, lumpy, loping bodies. They all looked like my sons. Like dear puppies. Not like potential lovers.

So then I eyed the middle-aged, baggy-assed, wearily balding, bespectacled men—the divorced men, the widowers, the husbands of others. Their sad, lined faces. Their bad posture. Their middle-aged guts. Their shoes trodden down at the sides. Their terrible hats. Their weary jeans. Their passé sweaters. Their pitifully jaunty leather bomber jackets that made them look like loser idiots. And they already had wives; or they had girlfriends; or they got dumped and were desperate; or they never got married and they were fussy and strange; or they were gay but didn't know it; or they were gay and did know it but didn't want anyone else to know it; or they were gay and they knew it and they wanted *everybody* else to know it; or they were heterosexual but they didn't actually like sex all that well; or they were embarrassed about it; or they weren't good at it; or they never liked it much and now they didn't have to do it anymore, thank God; or they couldn't get an erection; or they never really could get an erection; or they used to get an erection and now they could still get an erection but they just couldn't come.

But the main thing was that none of them were him. He was the one I was used to. He was the one I knew.

And without him I was just another woman alone. Drying up as I aged, alone in my bed.

All that winter I walked on the steep shore at Rice Point where the rocks pile up in a heap. The terrain shifting, the shape of the incline shifting with each storm that hurled its wild waters on the shore.

It was a cold day—midwinter. A Saturday. The wind pushing into me as I walked hard against it. I could hear the stones rub and rattle together with each wave. The sound of them clattering together reminded me of something—the sound of the bones in my back as I turned in the bed all alone.

I'd loved having a man in my life. It made me feel legitimate—a true grown-up. And it made me feel as if there were a buffer between me and the dark. That no matter what happened to me in the world, there was someone, someone—not my parents, not my children—but someone outside of myself—who had chosen me, who cared about me. Who would always be there.

I loved having a boyfriend, even though he wasn't always a perfect boyfriend, and I wasn't so perfect myself, sometimes. Though we rarely fought, there was often, between us, a low-level criticism. I didn't like the way he looked sometimes. Wanted him to trim his nose hair, his ear hair, his eyebrows. He hated when I suggested that. Was all fussy and made angry remarks. *I like my eyebrows! I like these pants!*

I thought it was my job. That that was what women did for men—kept them hair-free. Men somehow didn't seem to be aware of hairs sprouting out here and there all over them like wild tentacles. Weren't women in charge of gently reminding them? *Honey, you've got hair growing out of your nose. You've got hair growing out of your ears. You've got hair growing* off *of your nose.* That was the worst. Hair on the nose. Dark black, stiff—growing out and then curving down, unnoticed. How could he not notice it?

And all the blotches and the marks of life. Wasn't I supposed to be the one to tell him? Wasn't I supposed to be the one to keep him looking good? To check on his sun spots to see if they were melanoma. To give him nice shirts, nice sweaters to replace that favorite sweater or that old T-shirt with the saying on it he got back in the seventies and still wore—*Keep Watching! I might do a trick!*—that for some reason he thought was hilarious. Why hadn't he caught on to the fact that it no longer fit him? Why hadn't he caught on to the fact that he looked like shit in it? I thought I did a pretty good job of that. Encouraged him when he looked nice. Complimented him when he wore the navy sweater. Gently did not compliment him in the Mayan-looking wooly mud-colored sweater with the flouncy sort of trim at the bottom and the zigzag design.

I thought I did a pretty good job.

But maybe I let *myself* go? Maybe *I* was the one who looked lousy. Maybe *I* was the one—with my dopey stretchy corduroy Lands' End pants too big in the seat—who looked terrible. Maybe *I* was the one. Maybe I should have made more of an effort, worn better clothes, more glamorous underwear. Maybe I should have been prettier.

Maybe I should have had a new wardrobe, a sleeker body, a

better haircut, neater eyebrows myself, a different birth date, a different sell-by date, a different face.

One day last summer, six months after the breakup, I was driving home from Bangor. On the way I passed Expectations, a clothing shop I almost never went into, and on a whim I turned the wheel, cut across two lanes of oncoming traffic, parked in front of the store.

A bright floaty floral dress in the window had caught my eye. A girlish summer dress. The kind of dress I used to wear, when I was younger.

I walked out of the hot car into the cool air of the store. The carpet hushed my steps and all around me the women shopping, the women working there, all seemed absorbed in quiet positions of fashion study. The one holding a cream-colored shirt out before her, considering it. The one at the counter folding a beautiful blue-and-green scarf. It was quiet and eternal in the clothing store—the stacks of sweaters, the racks of blouses, the shoes arranged one by one on the far wall, the corridor leading off to the dressing rooms with their heavy, dark red curtains. The faceless manikins, the sparkling mirrors.

I walked past the dark and sober colors already arrived for fall. Their russet colors did not attract me: olive, cranberry, and brown. I wanted summer colors still. I wanted summer dresses, soft yellow cardigans, playful Capris. Wanted strappy sandals, painted toenails, tanned bare legs. I wanted to flip down the sidewalk with a bunch of flowers in a green paper cone. I would not be fifty-one in the scene I was imagining. I would be some timeless age in some ageless time. Twenty-seven, maybe, or thirty-five. My hair would be longer, too, and it would be loose and light. I'd be wearing dark glasses.

"Can I help you?" A young woman glided forward.

"That dress in the window—do you have it in a six?"

"The blue one?"

"No, the one with the flowers. I think it had green in it, and yellow. Maybe pink?"

I couldn't remember. It was the soul of the dress I remembered, not the details.

"Oh!" The woman went off toward one side of the broad room. "I'll see if we have it."

I walked over to another long rack of summer clothes, picked out the summeriest of all. White chopped-off pants, a yellow linen shirt, a lime green sweater. Everything must be like that, for what was left of summer.

"This one?"

The girl was back. She was so young, I thought. Could be my daughter. How old must she be? Nineteen? Twenty-two? Some tiny number. She held out the dress to me.

It was beautiful, hanging there in its flowered simplicity.

"Yes, that one."

"Shall I put it in the dressing room for you?"

"Yes, and could you put these things in, too? Thank you."

I felt assured, expansive, wealthy. I could buy anything I wanted. I had the money. Money I had earned myself dollar by dollar, day by day, chunk by chunk, those wonderful chunks of cash I carved out of my employment. I could buy anything I wanted—maybe a pair of sandals to go with the lime green sweater, the white pants.

This fragrant, happy train of thoughts moved through my mind as I moved through the store—colors, fabrics, the feel of a light silk blouse against my hand.

I found a black sweater folded with other sweaters in a bright knit jumble on a table. Went with everything. Black with white—very sophisticated! Black with red—exciting! Saturday night! A pair of tight Capris with roses printed on them. "Too much?" I asked the bored young woman in the beaded sweater.

"I think they'd be great on you!" the girl gushed falsely, but I took them anyway.

A soft, green boatneck sweater. On sale, only twenty-seven dollars. A pair of cement-colored linen pants. They'd go with anything, I thought purposefully and practically in that way we do when we're determined to spend far too much money. They'd go with anything, and I could wear them, I thought judiciously, into the fall.

I wanted to buy everything. The things the young girl took away off to the shadowy corridor of the dressing rooms, the new things which I also piled into my arms. Abundance. Harvest. The full fruits of summer. *Their branches bending down*, he had once written to me, *heavy with fruit*—describing the raspberry bushes in his back pasture.

I wanted to slap my credit card down on the counter and say, *I'll take it all;* to feel that breathless little thrill as the salesgirl added it up. And then I wanted to watch as she folded each item—the flowery dress, the yellow blouse, the boring yet practical linen pants—each item in its own sheaf of purple tissue paper; as she layered them into two big bags, the expensive kind of shopping bags with the store name scrawled casually in big gold letters on the side. I would walk out, encumbered, swollen with purchases, sated at last, into the hot day, and my own hot car and drive away with the radio on—loud music and the bright, hot sky!

But in the dressing room a different reality awaited me—that little room so full of clothing. I closed the heavy curtain and stood there, staring at the kill. I felt exhausted. Carefully I lifted down the flowered dress. I'd start with this one, and, as is always the case, this one dress would determine how all the shopping went.

I have learned, over the last ten years, not to look at a dressing room mirror unless I'm fully clothed. Not to turn my back on the mirror, lest it attack me. With clothes on, I look all right. Or in my own mirror in my bedroom, in the kind lamplight, and especially if I stand side-to, I look pretty good, especially since I've been working out at Curves. My belly isn't exactly flat—but it doesn't stick way out. My breasts have never been high. They are lower now, but still full, and the skin of my shoulders, my back, my belly, still smooth and lovely. And my legs—they always tell me this—my legs are great.

But in the merciless stare of the dressing room mirror I am not myself. Not the self I am at home. Not the self I want to be. So I've learned not to look.

With my eyes shut, I slid the light dress down over my body, buttoned it up, and, at last, looked into the mirror.

The dress was really beautiful. The flowers and the leaves entwined. The buttery color of the background. Beautiful. It fit me well—I really had gotten thinner—all that sorrow-induced starvation had paid off. I was in good shape. I turned halfway to see myself from the side and saw that the dress didn't tug or pull. It came in at my waist, flared out over my hips in a good way. I swayed a little, side to side, and the dress swayed with me, half a beat behind. It was a dress I could wear walking down a summer sidewalk carrying a woven summer bag. A dress I could wear sipping tea at an outdoor café deep in a fascinating conversation. It was a dress that would make me feel lovely and effervescent and light and beautiful—if I were twenty years younger. Because here, standing here, honestly, alone, before the mirror, arms by my sides, no audience, all pretense gone, I saw myself as the self I was. The self I had become. The lines in my face. My hair, no longer a wild carefree flourish of curls, but stiff, dyed, sticking out. My skin too tanned too many times. My slenderness only boniness now. I looked like someone wearing someone else's dress. I looked like a wrong doll with the wrong dress—this dress went to the doll with the blonde hair, with the arms akimbo, with blue eyes alight—not the middle-aged doll with her dull underwear. Not me.

"Everything all right in there?" the girl called in to me.

"Everything's fine," I said.

David turns off the engine. The music's cut off midchord. He makes that sort of half sighing, half grunting sound that I remember. The same sound he used to make when he came.

All is quiet.

He seems to be just sitting there. This is the time when, if he's known I'm back here all along, he will address me. I steel myself for his words.

So, Virginia, I imagine him saying. *What are you doing back there? Are you ready to come out?*

But he doesn't say anything, and Br'er Virginia she lay low.

Still he sits there.

I am frozen in position, afraid to move.

Then he reaches over the back of the seat to grab the bag from Rogerson's, opens the door, and heaves himself up and out. And he never even sees me, doesn't notice the lump under the mackinaw, but slams the door and goes off.

Deep under the pile of clothing and backseat debris, I lie still. Like a dead bird under the leaves in the late fall. Like a frog deep under the murky ice frozen in winter. I wait.

I hear a door open and a screen slam shut. He is in the house.

I wait.

A car goes by on the road far away and then another. I wait a little longer. But I feel stiff; I need to stretch, so finally I get up, pushing the coat and the sweaters aside.

It's late afternoon. The last light shines on the fields, on the pond that lies nearly next to his house. The Jeep's still warm, but I'm sure it's chilly outside. The light is so beautiful. If we were still together, if I had gone into the house with him, I would have said, *Oh, come on, let's walk down to the harbor!* and we would have walked down to the harbor together in this last golden light from the day. We might have talked about the quality of the late-September light. The way it's more golden than other times of the year. We might have gossiped about somebody, or we might have just walked. I with my arm through his, the way we always used to walk, back when we were together.

I look through the windows of the Jeep, at the pond, at the road, at the sky with the changing light as the day moves toward sunset, the almost greeny tinge in the southwestern sky, the band of clouds lit from beneath by the setting sun, and it all looks like a painting or something—unreal.

But now what am I supposed to do? I can't stay in here forever. I hadn't really thought it through, never thought about arriving anywhere. I just got in the truck. I didn't have a plan, I just got in, hid myself, and here I am—at his house that I know so well, that I don't know at all anymore. It's been almost a year since I was last here.

Maybe I could just go knock on the door. I've imagined it so often—arriving here at his house, in remorse, in reconciliation, in anger—having it out with him, wooing him back to me, telling him off. But no. What could I say to him? He doesn't want me here. What if he's cold and distant the way men can be cold and distant when they don't want to acknowledge what you both know is true? *Oh well, I don't remember,* they say. Or, *I don't know what you're talking about.* And they do know. You know they do. Only maybe they don't.

I could just go back to Sinclair. Walk part of the way, or hitchhike. It's not that far. Someone would pick me up.

But that seems flat to me, and ordinary, since I've come all this way. I might as well go in. See what it's like now in his house, in his life. See him, finally. I want to know, once and for all, who he is, who he ever was. The kind man I thought he was, who loved me, and who would never leave me or hurt me? Was he the sad lonely man who just couldn't cope? Was he a liar all along, and a creep? I want to investigate him. I want to get in there, to scout around, to finally be done.

Invigorated by these thoughts, I prepare to exit the truck. I have to do this right. I'll have to be very, very quiet. I'll have to get out when nobody's driving by—somebody who might look down the driveway and see me, who might then call him up: *Hey, Dave, think I saw someone getting out of your truck just now. Looked like that gal you used to go with—what was her name? Indiana? Kentucky? Some state wasn't it? Down South?*

And David, in this scenario, looks startled, then gets a pensive, inward look as he hangs up the phone. He did think he heard something funny in the backseat, driving home from Sinclair. He thought at the time he was imagining it, but maybe it really happened. *Hmmmmm.* Thinks about it. *Hmmmm.*

Goes out and discovers me hidden in the garage, clutching a half-eaten bag of pretzels in my nearly frozen fist. His face wide open with disbelief. His face distorted with rage. His face softened with love. His face murky with regret. His face.

I better wait until the coast is clear.

No one on the road. No cars approaching. I grab a sweater for extra warmth—I may be crazy, but ever practical—get the pretzels (no sense starving), and climb out. For a moment comes the *ding! ding! ding!* He's left his keys in the ignition. But then I'm out and I scurry into the garage with its huge door half open and the silent, unused car within.

It's a 1959 Cadillac Coupe de Ville—heavily finned, a once glamorous car. It will start, but it doesn't really go. He was always going to fix it up—described the summer drives we'd take Downeast—but he never got around to it and it has just sat here for years. But now, in the dusky interior of the large and cluttered garage, the car looks welcoming and kind; those soft plump seats. That generous shelf of tufted fabric. I climb in gratefully, lie down, gnaw on a large stale pretzel for a while, pull his sweater around me, and smell his smell. The garage is quiet, moody, dark, and tranquil. I'll just stay here and wait until he goes away and then I'll case the joint. Just once. Just look around. And then I'll leave. I'll get back up to Sinclair somehow. I'll never come back here again. I'll never bother him. Maybe I won't even see him ever again. But I will know more than I know now. At least I'll know something. And maybe, I think,

I'll leave some sign for him, some token. Not a note, but some-thing. I'll have to think about this. Something only he would recognize. I have to think.

I think these things, await the sound of him coming out of the house, getting into the truck, driving away. I gnaw a pret-zel, pull the sweater close, then realize, with a sort of dazed, glad surprise, that I am falling asleep. I feel, for the first time in months and months—I feel safe.

8

When I wake I'm lying in the backseat of the Cadillac and it's pitch black in the garage. Something woke me: the sound of someone closing the garage door tight. I hope he didn't lock it. I could starve in here. I sit up in the big, padded backseat of the old car. Outside I can hear the sound of the truck door opening and then slamming shut, the engine starting, and the sound of him driving away.

It's dark, a little cold now, and it will get colder.

I feel around for the door handle, open the car, and get out. Slide my hand along the smooth flank of the car, and then walk forward, arms outstretched toward the garage door, until I can feel the rough surface with my fingers. I bend down, try to pull it up. It gives just half an inch before it catches. It's locked. He's locked me in.

Now what?

Nobody knows I'm here. It's late September, already. It could go down below freezing tonight. The only way out is to hammer away at the door until somebody hears me and rescues me—if they even hear me. And if they do hear me—and who is *they*?—some random person who happens to be lurking about in David's driveway? Somebody walking by on the road who has really really acute hearing? And if they do hear me and break down the garage door, what would they think? They'd stare at me. *Are you okay?* would be the first thing they'd ask me. The second thing: *What were you doing in here?*

What indeed?

I yank hard at the garage door, but there's no further movement. There must be a window. Isn't there a flashlight? I feel my way along the wall. It's covered with tools hanging from big nails: a rake, an old saw, and a tennis racket. I bump my hip against a lawn mower. It's full of the clutter of years, this old garage. Full of his history, not mine.

I can turn the car headlights on—just for a moment—to see if there's a way out. I'm pretty sure he's left the keys in it; he always does. He's so proud of living in Maine, where you can leave the keys in the car. And besides, he locks the garage, so why would he lock the car as well? I reason these reasons, stumble back to the car, open the front door, slide in, and yes, there's the key. I turn it and the car starts with a kind growl. I feel around—a bunch of thick knobs on the dashboard. I pull out one of them and hear the rusty creak of dry windshield wipers wiping vainly at the dusty glass. Push that knob in and try another one and the lights go on. Just for an instant, before I shut them off. Someone looking down the drive might notice. In the brief light I've seen the rubble of the possessions that surround me: furniture, an unused kayak, some boxes, an old college trunk, a chair or two with broken legs, a rocker. But what did I expect to see? His old wife and discarded girlfriends? The various people he's shucked off? Deflated somehow, like the abandoned wet suit hanging from a peg. Their faces, like old rubber Halloween masks, empty, drooping? It's just old stuff in here. But where's the window?

I put the lights back on and look around. There's a window off to the left. It's kind of high, but I think it will open. If I stand on something. But I will need light.

I leave the headlights on and drag a table over to the window, climb up and get it open, turn the headlights off, and wait. I hear a car go by. Then there is silence all around as I creep back, sure-footed now, across the cement floor, up onto the table, climb over the sill, and leap right out into the bright cold night air, feeling the rush and clarity of that one brief midair moment, moving out and up and, finally, down, to where I fall onto the ground, roll once, lie still—the cold damp grass beneath me, sound of the stream nearby, and up above and all around the bright, bright far-off stars!

No car goes by and from down the road I hear a dog bark once in a lonely way. Although it is only the end of September, already it's like winter in his town. The summer people gone. The roads all quiet after dusk. No wonder he got lonely here, living alone in his big house, waiting for me.

David's cellar door is always unlocked. It's dark and damp and dank in here. Piled with bags and boxes to take to recycling. Just inside the door I can smell the smell of old newspapers bunched together, their pages sticky with the autumn damp. He's left a light on in here, and the cellar looks exactly the same as it did a year ago—or whenever I was here last; before the breakup. The washer and dryer heaped with shirts he says he's going to iron.

His workbench with a clutter of tools and little tubes of glue and half-started projects. I used to think, when we were first together, that he was the kind of man who could fix things, but he isn't. He's the kind of man who takes things to be repaired, but not until after he's left them for a good two years on his workbench intending to fix them. At that point he either takes them to be repaired or simply throws them out. So the wooden box that belonged to his grandfather. So the drawer from the little table beside his bed.

I remember this smell. The mildewy, damp, sad smell that was the smell in his truck, the smell of his jacket. The smell of his hair sometimes. The smell of his life. A lonely, damned, damp, sad, wintery, abandoned smell. The smell of loneliness. The smell of neglect. The smell that he inhabited and resented and presented to me.

The cellar steps are steep and narrow. It's an old house. He is proud of it. He told me how much he loved his house, complained about how little time I spent in it. That was in his final letter, after the night when he said he needed a break, before I understood that meant a permanent break. A total break. A silence. Before I understood all that, I had sent him an e-mail in which I tried to say everything I felt but which seemed, months later, as I reread it, a thin thing, a small thing, a twig of a thing—too kind, too soft, too understanding.

Later I thought I should have yelled at him—at least on

paper, since that night I did not yell. I should have hurled accusations. Instead I only said that I was sad. That I felt *some responsibility* for our breakup. That I hoped we could recover something from all we'd shared, as if his leaving were some sort of terrible tornado that had ripped through our houses and had broken everything, sent all our possessions, all the memories of the last ten years in all directions. Through the windows. Chairs flying, glass smashing, the sink itself. Dishes whirling out of the shelves. Tables. Lamps. The little bedstand with my book, my glasses—gone.

In my letter I assumed we would be talking, that we had begun a conversation about what was wrong and what we might salvage. Out in the yard, standing surrounded by the wreckage of our lives—but standing together, looking at the broken chair, the pile of crockery, the shards of glass in the drive.

Look! I would say to him. *Look! This is all right!* And I would hold up a plate—one plate—a blue one maybe, or one of the old ones that had belonged to his great-aunt. The ones with the dragonflies on them that scared me a little to eat from—to see their elongated insect bodies, their elegant wings emerge from under the mound of potatoes, the broccoli, the slices of pink ham.

And he would turn his head in that slow camel way and look at the plate and, if I were lucky, and if his mood were not too grim, he might even smile. We would have a plate to eat from, with a dragonfly on it. And maybe there would be a glass or two, a cup, a desk, a chair.

•••

But it wasn't like that at all. After the night when he told me he needed a break, when I still didn't understand what he meant by that, then there was only silence.

I didn't call him. I wrote him that one e-mail. I got his reply. How could I call him?

He didn't call me. He didn't seem to be concerned about me anymore. After all those years of caring so much about me. Of the tide coming in and staying. Of holding my hand at the movies. Of lying together in bed. Of breathing one another's breath, of holding one another tight, of knowing one another's children and one another's lives, and the details and minutiae and menus of one another's days. After consulting one another about everything from which heavy jacket to take to London to how much to pay for a car—after all that. After all of the tears and the singing in the car and the walks and the quiet afternoons by the fire—after all that, he was gone.

But now I can rediscover him. Investigate my loss. Girl detective. A spy in the house of Dave. Now, I think, as I go up the narrow cellar steps which I have bumped up with my overnight bag, which I have descended after a weekend of love. Now I will find something out. Something that will explain it all to me. Define him, finally. Something that will help me, finally, to let him go.

The kitchen is the same. Still the same place mats I gave him four years ago at Christmas. Bright colored—oranges and reds, blues and greens, with big flowers painted on them. He said that he loved them. I remember his face as he opened the package. And that year, didn't I give him a mug as well? With a penguin on it? And didn't I give him, I must have given him, the same soap we gave one another every year that smelled so strongly of lemon that you could smell it right through the wrapping paper, right through the box. *What could this be?* he'd said, smiling.

There's the usual clutter on the counter—a half-empty bottle of wine, his coffeemaker, a pile of bills and newspapers, a list scribbled on a pad. The lamp's on in the corner, beside the rocker where he said he liked to sit. I didn't quite believe him. I didn't think he sat in that rocker, reading his book, in the evening. I thought he mostly sat in the living room and watched television, now that he had the satellite dish. Sports. Some stupid sitcom. The news.

The rocking chair looks especially empty tonight. It's not all that comfortable. I'd tried sitting in it, over there by the window in the corner where it's kind of chilly, as he bustled about the kitchen fixing some meal or other, putting things away, in that light, bouncy, self-conscious way he moved. There on the shelves, the plates with the fancy dragonflies. There the cupboards with their flowered handles. I remember when he chose those handles. I remember when he chose this floor. It was early on in our relationship and we looked at the various samples together. *What do you think?* he asked me. *What do you think? Do you like these?* Maybe he was thinking that we would be living together in this house, though I always told him no, that I would never move. But people hear what they hear, not what you tell them. He always assumed eventually I'd live here with him.

I move now from room to room in his house. Am I hungry? I wonder as I pass the brown refrigerator. *Why brown?* I asked him once. *Oh, Joan liked it,* he told me. His ex-wife. He blamed her for a lot of the decorating faux pas in his house. The black bathroom sink and Jacuzzi. The wallpaper in the living room. Her fault.

I open the brown refrigerator. I am hungry, but as always, nothing appeals to me. Half-full jars with sticky mouths. Pickles. Olives. Some kinds of odd chutneys and mustards. He used to get angry when I'd say, *But there's nothing to eat!* He'd say there was plenty to eat, but there wasn't. Old eggs and packages of butter, jam with a crust on top. The rest of a casserole. Cheese. The crackers on the pantry shelves were always stale and tucked back in with a rubber band around them, like an old lady would do. Mostly he went out, or he took me out. He loved food but he also hated it, resented that here he was, a sixty-year-old man, still cooking for himself. Resented me for not living in his house with him, fixing him meals, bustling about in his alien kitchen. Delicious aromas floating out the door to his study where he would be sitting, he imagined, with a nice glass of Scotch, reading some important papers at his desk.

His desk is still a mess. There the photographs of his granddaughter. There the toy zebra that I gave him on top of his computer. I've gotten rid of everything that reminded me of our relationship, but, evidently, he has not. He probably just forgot it was there.

One of the last times I was here, I came into David's study. Was it early in the morning? Had I spent the night? Was I barefoot? Did I have a cup of coffee in my hand? Maybe he was in the kitchen doing something. Maybe he had gone back upstairs. I came into the study and I looked at the familiar jumble—the heaps of papers on his desk, the little zebra, the photographs of his granddaughter. There was something wrong, but at first I didn't know what it was.

"Hey!" I yelled in to him. "Where's my picture?"

"What?"

His voice was muffled. He was in the kitchen. Maybe he hadn't heard me right.

"My picture! The one with the hat. The one you look at."

He made a disagreeable sound, I remember. One of his sort of groany, grumpy noises that meant *Oh God, more of this from her.*

"David?"

"What?" Now he sounded really irritated. Interrupted in some important work—like maybe putting the toast in the Toast-R-Oven, or pouring the juice.

"Where is it?"

He came into the study. Glanced around, as if he were looking for it.

"I don't know," he said finally, still in that irritated way. "I don't know, Virginia. It's around here somewhere."

•••

But weren't other photographs missing as well? Weren't the ones in his bedroom gone? And then, when I asked about them, didn't they magically reappear the next time? And why didn't I think that was strange? Why didn't I think that was just a little peculiar? That he would have put away the photographs that he had all those years, that he had looked at every day, that I had seen, when I visited, like talismans—that picture of the two of us back to back in the island field. Whenever I saw it I re-membered exactly how the grass had felt. The strong warmth of his back, the sun upon us. And the other picture, the two of us hugging at the garden over the river. Our faces hidden, our arms tight around one another. Where was that one? But I didn't think it was weird, for some reason. I didn't question him when he said, *I don't know.* I didn't question him because I trusted him so much. I trusted him completely. I thought he was the one man, of all the men I had known, the one man who would never leave me, who would never lie to me. Who would never hurt me. Who would always be there.

Now, of course, the photograph really is gone. I sit at his desk and stare at the image on his computer—the flying stars disap-pearing, moving forward, more coming, more going away.

I glance over the rubble of his desk—the piled-up papers, the bills and letters, and one thing catches my eye—a notecard with a typical Maine scene on the front: boat, water, moun-tain. A colorful print of a second-rate watercolor. One I would never send.

I flip it open.

Dave, it says—a woman's writing. *I loved our sail. What a day! Our time together is so special. I will miss you until I'm back again. Love, L.*

L? *L?*

And, *special?* Who actually says that, except if they're joking? L, evidently. He would have laughed at that; we would have made fun of it together. But now here it is on his desk. It isn't dated. I don't know when he received it. He has every right now to see a woman named L. To take her sailing. To receive cheesy cards from her with boring sentiments. Every right.

Did you have affairs when you were married?

   Yes.

Tell me about them.

Oh, that was a long time ago, he would say.

But then, sometimes, he would tell me. He seemed to sort of like recalling the subterfuge, the excitement, of his adultery. He said he was ashamed of it. He said it was because he was so unhappy in his marriage, but he couldn't leave because of the kids. He had to stay.

And I said, *You wouldn't ever do that to me, would you?*

It even became a joke between us. When he'd tell me about some woman that he met, I'd say, "Are you having an affair with her?" And he'd say, "Come *on,* Virginia." It was one of our jokes, because I knew he'd never do that. Not to me.

Now I want to look all through his desk, to dig into all the drawers, his bills, read his bank account statements. I want to know everything about him. I want to know the real truth. He was always vague about how much money he had. Now I can find out for sure. I want to read letters from his old girlfriends. I want to find out how many women he was seeing while he was with me, how many times he pretended to be somewhere he wasn't, how many times he lied.

I want to open his computer and search his e-mail messages. Are mine still in there? Or have I been deleted? Are Natalie's? Are L's?

I would like to go through his trash can, read his files, plunder the messy piles on his desk. What other secrets does he have? What else is there?

But he could come back at any time. And I want to look in every room before I go.

I slide the card with the sentimental sailing scene back under the pile. I push the papers back the way they were, straighten the picture of his granddaughter so that she looks down kindly at me, as she used to, back when I was Grandma Ginny and David's family was my family, too.

9

I remember the day David's granddaughter was born. When he called me up, he sounded like the man I'd fallen in love with—excited, happy, delighted with life, not the sour, sad man he'd become.

This man was kind and happy. Loved me, loved his family. Loved his son, his pretty daughter-in-law, his wonderful new granddaughter.

We flew out to England a few days later to be the first of the long trooping line of grandparents to meet little Isabel.

She was beautiful. When I held her—so small! so light!—tucked in her blanket, I felt as if I were holding one of my own babies. Beth's face was soft with the softness of motherhood. She was nursing, and she had that smooth, inward, slightly dazed expression. We all crammed into Beth and Parker's tiny apartment and took turns holding the baby, took turns staring at the baby.

David and I walked through the streets of London restored to one another. In the old hotel where we stayed, we held each other as if we were the new parents, lay in the bed talking about all the things we would do with her when she got older. I was sure this was the beginning of the best part of our lives together.

If only we'd met ten years earlier, David used to say, we could have been parents together. When we started going out, his kids were already grown and mine were stalky preteens. Early in our relationship we talked about what it might be like to have a baby together. How different it would be for both of us.

He was a grown man after all the wobbly boys I'd gone for. A grown man with white hair and a house of his own and an antique car in the garage. A man with a business degree who owned a company, a suit, who even had, he showed me once, standing in the spare bedroom one chilly spring morning—a tuxedo. He opened the closet door and drew it out—bagged in its long gray plastic bag.

"I haven't worn it in a while," he told me. "Not much call for a tuxedo in Maine."

"I bet you look great in it," I told him.

And then—and I remember this so clearly, as if it just happened, just a moment ago—he carefully hung the suit back in the closet, turned to me, put his arms around me, and he kissed me, standing there. I was wearing one of his old flannel shirts, just out of bed, he was in his pajamas—and when he kissed me, I felt completely content.

How would it have been—how would our lives have been different if I had gotten pregnant, back when we were still so wonderful to one another?

One time I thought I might be. We were sitting in the front of his truck. I had called him and said I needed to talk to him, and he had come and picked me up at work.

We drove outside of Sinclair, down to that place by the river.

I was nervous.

"So I can take a test tomorrow. It'll be three weeks," I said.

And he didn't do that thing men do when women tell them that they might be pregnant. When they look startled, caught, then swiftly change their look of horror to another look, a more acceptable look, of cautious joy. He made only one look, and it was a good look.

"I don't know why you're scared," he said. "I'm not scared. I think it's wonderful."

And he had that same look now, in London, when I sat holding the baby in his son's apartment. I smiled down at Isabel. I felt old; my skin so worn and wrinkled in comparison to the smooth, impossibly flawless skin of the child in my arms, in comparison to Beth's smooth skin, in comparison to my own skin when I held my own baby years and years ago. But, even so, I felt beautiful holding the baby. That light, light bundle in my arms. The tiny fingers and the little face.

We went over to England every few months to visit. That was when we were happiest together, during the last couple of years. It was as if we did have a child of our own. A child we both loved, that we both had known since birth. We talked about her—what she had learned to do since our last visit. When she was a little bigger we took her to the park together, helped her on the swing, the slide; she was our grandchild.

Of course we loved one another's children, though his grown children had mixed feelings about this new woman in their father's life, and my surly teenage daughter resented him, made fun of him, and finally forgave him, got used to him, said even, *Oh, he's not so bad.* My son liked him but also thought he was slightly ridiculous with his hats and his funny accents and his old-man ways. But we loved one another's children and remembered their birthdays and patched together our approximated families at holidays in one another's houses. But this baby, this time with the baby, was something special. Something bigger. Something that made our own union seem more real. Now we were grandparents together. Now we were finally wed.

"Do you think we could ever get married?" he asked me. We were lying in bed together, both on our backs, in the high-ceilinged room in the old hotel where we stayed. Outside the light English rain fell down. We were waiting until it was time to go see the baby. It was the last day of our visit there. Isabel was only two years old.

He had asked me and asked me for so many years, but he never gave up on his question and though I always said no, now I said no regretfully and I said no with a certain longing and I said no thinking, *Well maybe yes.* Maybe sometime. This is so sweet. He is so sweet. Our time together so sweet. Maybe yes. Maybe I could marry this man, though I thought I would never marry again. Maybe this man. Maybe. If it could be like this, with the rain and the baby and the bed and the tall ceiling above us. Gradually growing older together. Maybe yes.

I wasn't ready, I always told him. I wasn't sure I could ever be married again. But I always told him, *But keep asking. I like it when you ask me.*

When he asked me to marry him, his face got a certain look. I called it his restaurant face because it usually occurred in restaurants. He loved to go out to eat, to sit opposite me, with his food before him, with a glass of good wine. The bread in its little basket. The butter in its little dish. The candles.

He took my hands.

"You have such soft hands," he always told me.

I smiled at him. I felt beautiful, right then, and no longer exhausted, the way I was always exhausted in those days—by work, by my children, by life. We were in a restaurant, in New York, in London, in Sinclair, in Boston, and I was with the man I loved.

"You've got your restaurant face," I teased him.

He exaggerated it, made a big mooncalf face to amuse me.

"Will you marry me?" he asked.

I hesitated. What could I say to him? Would I ever marry him? Would I never marry him? I would marry him in a minute, if it could always be like this—if we could always be seated in a restaurant, a little dizzy from the wine, with the good food coming and none of the concerns of life pestering at us. If we could always be out and never be back in the house together— if none of the rest were true.

But all of it was true, and I knew it was true, and I knew that within a week of trying to share a house together I'd be ready to assassinate him. That though I was sometimes lonely, I also loved my solitary life. Kids finally up and out. The neat stark silence of my walls. The bed where I woke up in the morning alone.

Twenty years after my divorce, I still loved the feeling of sleeping alone—of dreaming my dreams through the kind slope of a winter night, tucked way over to one side with pillows and books piled up beside me, with all the sheets and blankets pulled close around me—and, in the bright morning, scissoring my legs in wide slides along the smooth sheets. It was mine, all mine, the bed. I lay on my back, ran my own hands over my own body. Didn't have to hear anyone trooping about. Didn't have to talk to anyone, have anyone snoring, breathing, farting their papery farts beside me. There was that, too.

And there was the quiet order of the morning: the coffeepot for one, the flowers on the sill, the newspaper spread out on the sunny table, and the day outside. My workday before me— orderly and sensible and full.

So, "Not now," I always said. "But thanks for asking."

And did he look relieved? Or was he sad? Or did he smile? Or was he angry? I didn't know. I didn't think about it. It was our exchange. The food arrived. And we were done with that.

But then, in London, on those visits when we went over to see the baby, I imagined that we could be married. We walked down the street together, went into the hotel restaurant, and I thought how we must look—the two of us in the booth together— two middle-aged Americans from Maine, in town to visit our grandchild. We probably looked like we'd been married for thirty years, the two of us. I knew he wanted his coffee right away. He told the waitress I would have mine later. We bickered over eggs companionably and wound up splitting the country breakfast, and *This is pretty good,* he told me happily.

I've seen the baby only one time since the breakup. Last spring, in April, when Parker and Beth came to New England on a visit. They called me, asked if they could come over.

"I'd love to see you," I said.

I made some cookies, and we had tea together at the kitchen table. Isabel was three now and looked very tall. She remembered my Rolodex and wanted to play with it, but she didn't really remember me, didn't want me to hold her and yelled and pulled away when I tried to kiss her.

"She's so grown up," I said, trying to be funny about it, but feeling hurt.

When Parker was in the other room, Beth looked at me across the kitchen table. "Are you all right?"

"Yeah, I'm all right," I told her. "It was a tough winter. But I'm all right, now that it's spring."

Seeing them made me want to cry. I couldn't let them know that. They were staying with David. They'd be going back there. He might ask how I was and I wanted them to say that I looked wonderful. That I was doing well.

So I didn't cry in front of them. Tried to hold Isabel, let her go, smiled ruefully at her squirming away, and they hugged me and I talked about going over to see them sometime and we all pretended that I really would.

But I could not imagine going back to London without David. Where would I stay? In the hotel where we used to stay together? That musty smell of roses, or some kind of soap, in the hallway. The tall wide stairs. The chocolate hearts on the pillow with the pink foil wrappers.

No, I wouldn't go back alone.

I sent Isabel a birthday present, a little wooden village. And in reply I got a card from Beth. *We miss you,* she wrote. But they don't miss me. Time has closed the space up over me, like something sunk into water. You see it fall through the bright surface, then the water closes over, and, in a little while, even the ripples are gone.

10

The living room looks the same. Same couch. Same unusable fireplace which he has often said he might convert to gas. Same empty eye of same rattletrap television. Same dull old armchair set at an improper angle. The little wooden table I gave him. The lamp. The paisley cushions. The stain on the rug. Same pictures on the walls: the charcoal still life—three gray lemons in a lopsided bowl. The solemn angry man. The weary nude. The same pictures I stared at for years wishing that, if he had to have art, he could at least have good art. That he could have pretty art on the walls, not this ugly stuff. But here it is. The drab inheritance from his parents. The dark line drawings and the charcoal and the dirty colors. *I like this art,* he'd say. He'd been huffy about it, liking his art. Liking his eyebrows. Liking his house, his cellar with its musty smell. Liking his Jeep. His pretzel box and his depression. Liking these dark sad drab things of his life and hugging them to him even as he blamed me for all of it.

I head for the stairs. He'll be home soon. I have to finish here. I might have half an hour left, at most.

I'm not sure how long it takes, dinner. If he's with somebody. If he's eating alone. If he's reading a magazine, sitting at the bar. If he's in a booth. If he's deep in conversation. If he's staring at somebody else with his restaurant face.

I'm not sure of anything, just that I have to see the upstairs.

Just that I have to look into his rooms. To see the bed. To see the shabby black-sinked bathroom and his clothes in the closet. To see if he's changed or not changed. To see if he even exists. To see who he is, who he was. To see how it feels to see his things.

Up the narrow stairs with their tan carpet. I make no sound.

The upstairs hallway, where he took the photograph of little Isabel sitting on the window seat holding a wooden boat in her hands. The front room where Parker and Beth stay, still full of Parker's stuffed elephants from when he was a little boy himself. The scary room full of old bills and piles of papers and files; tuxedo in the closet in its plastic bag. The guest bedroom, that used to be his daughter Sarah's room, with the four-poster bed and the beautiful quilt. The bathroom. He's got a different kind of soap now. Black. Those long green dense cakes of lemon-scented soap we used to give each other every Christmas do last for a long time but, evidently, they don't last forever.

I stand in the doorway of his bedroom. I see a dark shape on the bed and freeze. It looks like a person lying there. But it isn't, of course, just a dark sweater, and a pair of pants, thrown down on the old comforter that he used to pull up over me to keep me warm.

I go into his bedroom. There is the lamp and the pile of books by his bed. The pillows. The bureau at the far end of the room with its reassuring rubble of David things—the pile of coins, the little carved Indian elephant, the broken watchband, the wooden box. There the narrow shelf over the fireplace with the row of framed photographs. I look at them one by one: his father with Sarah and Parker when they were little, Parker and Beth, Isabel and Isabel and again Isabel. The new baby. Zach. There is no picture of me. Did I think there would be?

Did I really think he would still be displaying a picture of me leaning up against him in the sunny island field? Did I really think he would have that picture of me and my daughter smiling down from the Ferris wheel at the Bangor State Fair?

I don't know what I thought. I stare at the familiar pictures and the unfamiliar photographs. I imagine him standing here; taking down the pictures of me.

Summer 1992, early in our relationship. We were in his bedroom. It was warm in the room. We had woken up late.

"I want to show you something," he told me.

He opened one of his bureau drawers and from under the folded T-shirts, drew out two large photographs in heavy frames. One was a picture of his wife when they were first dating. She was seventeen, tiny, with a beautiful heart-shaped face and long hair. Standing on a wooden porch somewhere, holding a bunch of flowers.

"God!" I said. "She was so pretty!"

"Yeah." David looked at the photo, holding it out from him and studying the face of his ex-wife. "She was beautiful. I think she still is."

He laid the picture on the bed, and showed me the other one.

This one was a photograph of a family gathering. "My brother's wedding," he said. The family was all arranged in a line, the bride and groom in the middle. David and his wife off to the left. Her hair was cut shorter, and he had a beard. He was serious, looking away from the camera.

"How old were you?" I asked him. "You look really young."

"Oh, I don't know, about thirty-five, thirty-six," he said.

"You look so serious."

"We were very unhappy."

He used to tell me how they didn't speak. In the evening when the kids weren't there, in their big house in Pennsylvania—they did not speak. He would sit in the living room with his book. She would stay in the kitchen as long as she could, cleaning up from their supper. And they did not speak. He would wait, he told me, until she'd gone up to bed, until he thought she must be asleep, and only then would he finally go up, so he would not have to talk to her, not have to see her looking at him, so that they would not have to not make love another night in the same bed.

"How sad!" I said when he told me that. But secretly I wondered—*But why didn't you do something about it? Why did you stay like that? Why didn't one of you leave?*

I couldn't imagine staying in such a bad marriage. Waiting it out like a life unlived. Waiting it out like a bad bit of weather. Like a dreary rainstorm that will pass, will pass. Waiting it out for years.

"We wouldn't be like that," he always told me. But had he

thought it would be like that with the pretty girl in the picture? Standing on the porch with her flowers, smiling uncertainly into the camera? Hadn't he thought they would always love each other as they had loved each other at the start?

Love seemed uncertain and impossible. I would rather, I told him once, be away from him and missing him, than to be with him and wish I weren't.

Are those photographs still there? Still lying there together under the T-shirts in the third drawer down? Has he put my pictures in there with them? Or did he throw them out?

I threw out everything I could after he left.

The first thing to go was the big box of chocolates he gave me for Christmas. He was always giving me candy. Fancy Godivas in a puffy red velvet heart. Whitman samplers with their familiar yellow embroidery pattern on the box. Russell Stover from the drugstore with a map of the candies within: the nougat, the orange cream, the coconut, nut cluster, fudge.

Last Christmas, a week before the breakup, he gave me an enormous box of chocolates. Filled assortment—dark chocolate. My favorite. I would have one piece every morning after breakfast. Not just Sundays. The children were gone now; I didn't have to set a good example.

I kissed him. "Thank you, honey. I'm all set for months now."

Why did he look away? He was so strange lately, I thought. I thought it was the business deal he was working on. It wore him out with its uncertainty, its lack of resolution. I thought it was depression. He was so odd and nervous lately. But look what he'd given me! A beautiful pearl necklace with gold beads in between. The long slab of lemony green soap. The box of chocolates. How dear he was, and how essential to my life. I would be better. I would try harder. I would be a better girlfriend. I'd make him happy if it killed me.

But one week later, with only six pieces gone from the candy box, I hurled it into the kitchen trash, and threw his slippers in on top of it—which made it all the more revolting. Slippers! Garbage! Chocolates! Old Kleenex and eggshells of our love!

And since then I haven't been able to eat chocolate. A dark thing. Unpleasant, sweet and bitter in a bitter way.

After that, after I broke through the initial ice of my despair, it was easier to get rid of other things that he had given me or things that reminded me of him. The photographs of David on his boat with his handsome summertime face. Well tanned and happy with his ropes and charts. The picture that had stood on my dresser smiling at me in the bed for ten years, now face-down in the back of the linen closet under a pile of sheets. The photograph of David drinking coffee, sitting in a chair in my living room. The two of us in Canada on vacation. Standing together in London, holding the baby Isabel. All of those pictures are gone.

And so has he removed all trace of me? I can't see anything that might remind him of me. The little red heart pillow I gave him our first year. The dark green robe. What has become of the cranberry-colored pajamas—my gift to him last Christmas?

•••

I often gave him pajamas. He liked them and I liked to see him in them—the crisp blue pajamas with his monogram, which I gave him before our trip to the Bahamas. The striped blue-and-white ones from the department store in London that he wore and wore. The dark, handsome Black Watch plaid ones that reminded me so pleasantly of my father. Last December David had been hinting that he needed new ones, so I ordered a new pair of flannel pajamas from L.L.Bean.

It seemed like a good omen—that of all the hundreds of L.L.Bean Christmas phone operators I got the same man I had spoken with the year before when I ordered David's bathrobe. He remembered me, too.

"What are the odds?" he asked me. "What are the odds that you'd get me again?"

And—"Another present for your boyfriend? He's a lucky guy!"

We had a consultation about color. I thought gray at first but then, thinking how sad David had been lately, I thought gray might be dismal. He needed some stronger, more hopeful color. Not white. Nobody wears white flannel pajamas. And I didn't want plaid.

"What do you think of the cranberry?" I asked my new friend on the phone.

"It's very handsome," he said cautiously.

"And don't you think it's kind of a happy color?"

"Happy. Yes. I see what you mean," he said.

"I'll get them. Tall and—I guess medium. He's lost weight lately."

"Fine. And anything else? Anything for you?"

"No, he'll get something for me," I told him. "He always does."

But David hardly reacted when he opened the package and saw the new pajamas. They were even prettier than I expected— the color so deep, so true, so warm and cheerful. Christmassy without being the sort of thing you might get sick of by mid-February. Beautiful. Not a harsh and hearty blustery Santa red, but a deep heart dark red—permanent and warm and sort of sexy.

"Don't you like them?"

But he looked pensive; stared down morosely at the pajamas in their plastic bag.

"They're nice," he said at last. "Thanks, Virginia," and he kissed me.

I felt a little dart of the impatient fury I was trying not to feel today, on Christmas. We were moving out of the sad gloom of the past fall and toward a bright new year. I wanted everything to be nice again. The New Year! Christmas and the beautiful dark red pajamas! Chocolates and the lights on the pretty little tree. My sister Judy and her husband and my nieces would be here from Indiana for the weekend. Surely now his glumness would pass and we would be happy together again.

"Stay with me, Virginia," he had whispered to me, reaching

for me again after the sad failure of our love last night. "Stay with me. Hang on. I'll come back to you."

I open the bureau drawer now and there, still in the plastic L.L.Bean bag they came in—the beautiful dark red pajamas.

It was morning, the last day of December. It was cold but not brutal yet. The brutality would come in January, when it would get really cold.

I was at my desk. I was working on something on my computer. Writing something I had to write for work. Going over my notes for the talk to the young businesswomen: "How to Succeed in the Business World."

The phone rang. It was David.

Why was he calling me right now when he knew I was working? This was my working time, I thought, irritated. He should know better than to call me right now.

I picked up the phone, glaring a little at the caller ID.

"Hi," I said.

"Hi. Are we still on for tonight?"

What an odd question to ask! It was New Year's Eve! Of course we were still on. I'd made reservations at Chlöe's. I had planned what I'd wear—red sweater, the black velvet pants, and the pearls with the little gold beads.

"Sure. It'll be fun." Then—"Are you okay?" because his voice sounded kind of weird.

I didn't really want to know. He was never okay anymore. He

was always angry or sad these days. Something wasn't right.

"So we're going?"

Oh God.

"Of course. And we'll get up early and have a wonderful breakfast on New Year's Day," I told him. "I got lox."

I really had no clue, I thought later. I thought it was just his depression that made him sound so strange. I thought I could jolly him out of it, by offering special treats, by being friendly and bouncy and full of fun. All excited about the eggs and bagels. All delighted with the lox.

"Oh, so I'm spending the night?" he asked me.

What's with him? I remember thinking.

"Well, yeah!"

"Oh. Okay."

He was so weird. We'd been going together for ten years; spending the night at least once a week, and certainly every New Year's Eve. We were lovers. We were best friends. How odd he was. He seemed disoriented, lost. It must be his depression.

Just the other night he had told me again his life felt meaningless. I'd urged him, for the thousandth time, to get some help. He'd never gone to that appointment after all. *Something came up,* he'd said, *I couldn't make it.* The next day I e-mailed him the name of another therapist who was supposed to be pretty good. *If you want I'll call him and make the appointment,* I wrote. David seemed unable to do anything. I just couldn't understand the texture of it. His despair.

Later, of course, I would taste it myself. I would get my own bitter draft of it. The unendurable sharpness on the tongue.

But that came later.

That morning: "Well, of course you'll spend the night here, won't you?"

"I guess so."

"You can wear your new pajamas," I said coyly, thinking how it would feel to put my face against that lovely dark-cherry-colored flannel. That lovely rich dark color that I chose.

"What?"

"Your new pajamas. The ones I gave you last week for Christmas."

"Oh, yeah. I don't know. I think they're wet," he told me.

"Wet?"

"I put them in the washer," he said.

Later, I remember, I thought that was a weird thing to say. Wanted to answer—*Well, then put them in the dryer!*—but I didn't want to spoil this new year by starting it on such a sour, carping note. And I was excited about the prospect of winter— the sharp stark crystalline promise of January—the clear hard sky, the ice on everything, the concentrated glitter. It would be a good winter to work, I thought. I imagined myself getting up earlier and earlier each day—going to my desk. Coffee beside me. Working, working. Each task a hard bright gem. My thoughts clear, the way they can be clear in winter. My clothes severe, warm, sensible. Tight jeans and a thick knit sweater. Hat on and mittens and my big coat as I marched through the snowy roads of Maine. Along the riverbank. The path there hard and bright beneath my boots. The hard-packed frozen ground. The dirt in little ridges, once mud, now frozen there. Sharp creases hard with ice. The frozen puddles.

I would celebrate the winter this year—the outline of the trees against the sky. Black branches and the sky beyond. The hard, intrinsic bones of the world.

David would get better. It would start tonight and would begin tomorrow—the new day and the new year stretching forth.

11

I go to his closet. The high shelf towering with wooly stacks of sweaters. The slippers and the shoes below. The shirts on their hangers. The checked one I always liked. I take that shirt out and put my face against it.

"Can I come lean against you?" I would ask him. We were reading our books. We were sitting by the fire. We were watching a movie. There was a sad ending. It was winter. It was early in the spring. It was the fall. Year piled on year and season on season.

"Come here," he'd say and I would crawl down to his end of the couch and put my face against the front of his shirt and feel his warm chest. He'd put his arms around me. Push his face into my hair. His warm lips against my head, strong arms around me.

The dark blue bathrobe that I gave him is hanging on the inside of the closet door. Beneath it, I know, his belt. The good one that he rarely uses. Does he still have the furry slippers that he brought me from his trip to Finland? They were too big. I kept them here, so I could wear them when I visited. I look for them beneath his shoes, but they are gone. Did he throw them in the kitchen garbage the way I threw his out? Did he put them away in some dusty box in his attic? Did he give them to some other, larger-footed woman?

•••

New Year's Eve. I had been busy all day. Took a walk in the afternoon with my friend Rose.

"What are you doing for New Year's?" I asked her, though I already knew Rose was having an old friend over—Ray.

"Are you finally going to sleep with him?"

"No. I just don't want to. I like him. I love him, really. But I'm not attracted to him."

"Too bad. It would be so handy."

"Yes, but nope. Not this year, anyway. What are you and David doing?"

"Going to Chlöe's."

"Oooh-la-la."

"Yeah. I know. But all of a sudden I don't feel so good."

"What's wrong?"

"I don't know. It just came on. Maybe I'm getting a cold. I don't know."

"Well, you won't stay out late, will you?"

"No. I just don't feel good."

"Maybe you shouldn't go."

But I didn't want to let David down. And I thought how much he liked to go out to eat. How maybe tonight he'd be happy and he'd hold my hands and look at me with his restaurant face and he'd tell me how soft my hands were and how beautiful I was and how much he loved me and he'd probably ask me to marry him again. And then maybe all the rest of it—the bad mood, the weirdness, the forgetfulness—maybe all that would finally disappear. Maybe he would have gotten the Viagra as he said he would last time. Maybe he would bring me home and though he didn't have the dark red pajamas maybe he'd have some other pajamas or maybe no pajamas just his warm skin and mine and the bed around us like a big clean sea and he would hold me, and he would love me, and I would feel beautiful, stretched out on the bed beside him, beautiful and angelic on the last night of the year.

And maybe this last night would erase all the other nights—the sad nights and the bad nights that have lain between us like a weary pelt. Maybe this last night would be the beginning of the new time and I would see him in a new way and he would be darling to me again the way he once was so darling and I would know that I was darling, too, to him.

But I didn't feel good and so, finally, late in the afternoon, when Rose had gone home, I called David at his house and told him, "I don't feel so good."

"Do you want to cancel?" he asked me.

"I don't know. What do you think?'

"If you don't feel good . . ."

"Yeah, I don't. I feel sort of coldy," I told him.

"Well then, let's skip dinner."

"You don't mind?"

"It won't be any good if you don't feel well," he told me. "I don't care. Do you want to be alone?"

"No," I said, "I want you to come down. Don't you want to? We can have a fire. Don't worry, I won't breathe on you. I've got some good bread and some champagne and you could get a movie. We could just watch a movie."

And maybe, I thought, it would be a slightly dirty movie. A sexy love movie and he would lie on the green couch with me and we would drink the champagne and get a little tipsy and I would lean back against him and the movie would be uncomplicated and pleasant, and we would laugh at the funny parts, buoyed by the friendly fizz of the champagne, and I would feel his laughter in his chest and it would be easy again. Maybe he would touch me in the old way—in the old patterns that we had perfected over the years, and he would seem not shabby and sad and angry and moody—not contemptuous or contemptible, but loving and masterful and strong and handsome and powerful and tender, too, the way he always used to be.

And then we would make love, there on the couch by the fire and maybe we would tip over the champagne glasses, or knock over the lamp or something, something comical and friendly. And later we would go up to bed and burrow down into the covers together with the window just slightly ajar to let in the cold bright air of the first and last night of the year and there we would sleep.

I dressed in quiet, sexy clothes—the long brown snake of a skirt that he could slide his hands up under. The soft long stretchy red sweater that he had given me years ago. I wore stockings and my slip-off shoes and I made the fire and brought in some extra wood and got the champagne ready and a tray for the bread and cheese and some fancy black olives; grapes in a little basket, two champagne flutes, and I lit two candles on the mantelpiece and the quiet lamp that sent a golden glow across the room. The winter cold outside but in here warmth and amber light. The quiet sound of the fire, two dark red velvet cushions on the floor.

He called me from the movie store in Sinclair.

"What do you feel like seeing?" he asked me.

"What do they have?"

"I don't know."

He sounded confused, distressed, I could imagine him shaking his head hopelessly at the rows and rows of DVDs and videos—bright plastic boxes and the too-bright lights.

He was always confounded by the movie store. He would take his cell phone and stalk up and down the aisles, calling out the weary names in alphabetical order. He always sounded aggravated and exhausted when he did this. *You've seen that one, too? God, you watch a lot of movies,* he'd tell me. *Come on, give me another one,* I'd tell him and he would give me one name and then the next name and the next and I would listen to the titles and reject them one by one, or else he would say, *What's this one about?* and I would say, *I think there's killing in it,* and he'd say, *I don't mind a little killing,* and I'd say, *Not tonight,* and then he'd say, *What do you want then?* And I'd say I wanted something sweet and funny but not too sweet and not too funny and not gross. I didn't mind sad if it was just sappy sad, but no depressing sad ones. And not too dark.

What do you mean, dark? he'd ask me.

And I'd say, *You know what I mean. Not dark.*

Okay, he'd mutter. *Not dark. Not gross. Not full of killing. How are you with suspense?*

I like suspense.

Okay. So maybe something with suspense.

So I expected this sort of thing when he called me that New Year's Eve—that he would be reading off movie titles to me and I would be saying no way okay and he would say, *I already saw it,* and so forth, but he was quieter than usual. Just reading off the titles.

At last we decided *Chicago.* I'd already seen it, but he hadn't.

"You'll like the dancing. You'll like seeing Catherine Zeta-Jones's breasts," I told him.

"You sure you don't mind seeing it again?"

"No. It's great. It's perfect. I'll see you in a half hour."

"Okay," he said.

I felt kind of excited. I was glad we weren't going to Chlöe's after all. Glad I didn't have to get all dressed up and go out in the cold and spend too much money. This would be better: a cozy night with David by the fire. The real new year would begin tomorrow morning, when we would walk somewhere beautiful along the river and we would be hand in hand and bright-faced with the cold and we would feel full of wishes and good promise for the year to come.

12

I heard his Jeep approach the house, heard the slam of the truck door. His footsteps on the porch.

I heard the front door, stayed seated on the green couch by the fire.

"David?"

He didn't answer, but I heard him make that sighing sound he made, almost a groan, as if the world were a difficult place, as if the enormous task of coming up the steps and into the house had almost done him in.

"David? I'm in here."

I heard him putting his coat in the hall closet. The clank of hangers.

At last he came into the living room. He looked nice: brown corduroy pants, checked shirt, and navy sweater.

He didn't kiss me. That was the first thing. And he didn't sit down, either, but walked around the room.

"Come on, sit down," I told him. "Did you get the movie?"

He didn't answer. Funny. He could be so odd sometimes.

"You look great," I told him. He did look good. He was so thin lately.

He sat down, finally, at the other end of the couch. Turned his face toward mine. He looked serious.

"We have to talk," he said.

I looked at him, alert now. There was something.

"What?"

"I'm so unhappy, Virginia," he told me. "I'm unhappy and I'm angry all the time. I can't go on like this."

He started crying.

I made a little sound and moved forward to get close to him. I put my arms around him. He was crying so hard. He never cried, but now he was sobbing in my arms and his body felt funny: hard and tight and wooden, almost.

"Oh, David," I said. "Oh, honey, it's okay."

I hadn't realized it was this bad—his depression, his break-down, whatever it was.

He cried harder and I felt an enormous tenderness for him, and remorse. I moved closer, held him tighter, pulled him toward me. I loved this man. I felt everything in that moment—all of my strong feelings for him—how I loved him, how I pitied him, how I felt protective of him and protected by him, how I longed for him, how I felt tied to him. One with him. It was all there. All of it. Ten years' worth.

"And there's something else."

I could barely understand him. He was sobbing so hard now.

"There's something else," he said again. "I've been having an affair."

I leapt back from him as if he'd burned me. Stared at him. *What?*

He kept on crying, as if he didn't even notice that I'd moved away.

I was staring at him.

"What?"

"An affair," he repeated.

"For how long?" I wondered, later, why I asked that first.

"I don't know," he said. "About four months."

Four months. Later, that number, that stretch of time, became my touchstone. Became the number I obsessed over, searching back through my memory, back through my journals, for every moment of every day of those last four months. The times I couldn't reach him on the phone, the times he didn't want to stay over, the time he'd seen that movie and he said, "Oh, he'd gone with some friends from work." Signs and other signs. Obvious marks. Things I should have caught but didn't, because I wasn't looking. The bloodstains on the floor. *But I didn't think he'd ever do anything like that, Officer.*

"Four months?" I asked him now, so he could tell me no, he didn't mean that. I had heard it wrong.

I was still staring at him, but he wouldn't look at me. He had his eyes shut. He was crying.

"Why?" I asked.

"I wasn't thinking," he said. Then he stopped. Looked right at me. And in that look was everything. Everything just under his sobbing. Everything under his dithery confusion. Everything under his so-called depression. Under all of those looks was another look—a look of sheer hatred. And then he said distinctly, with no sign of tears, "Of course I was thinking. I knew what I was doing."

That was the clearest thing he said all night.

Later I couldn't remember exactly what we said. I remembered it was weirdly friendly, almost comradely. We talked for hours. I was, I realized later, in a kind of shock, so that I didn't say any of the things that I later wished I had said, or ask any of the questions that I later wished I had asked.

Is this because I wouldn't marry you?

Is this the same thing that was going on five years ago when you were acting so weird?

You bastard you bastard you bastard.

You pretend to be this caring, kind, befuddled man, but you're a liar.

You're a fake and a liar.

And, of course: *Were there others?*

But I didn't say any of these things. Instead I said random, oddball things, it seemed to me later. At one point, I remember, I asked him what the name of the woman he'd been seeing was.

"Natalie," he told me.

I didn't know if he was telling me the truth.

"Does she have big breasts?" I asked him.

He stared at me. But he, probably just as stunned as I was by this inappropriate response to his revelation, finally answered, "Not particularly."

"Does she have long hair?"

"Not real long, no."

"What color is it?"

"Brown."

And then I thought—well, if she just has brown hair, and she doesn't even have big breasts, then what's the point of it? What could she have? What would it be that would make that particular vagina, that pair of eyes, that set of lips, any better/different/sexier than the ones I've got?

"Is she young?"

"About your age," he told me. "Maybe a year or two younger."

So, why?

But he could be lying about this, too. About what she looked like. Who she was. Her age. Her name. She could be anybody.

Now we were playing twenty questions. I'd moved beyond animal, vegetable, or mineral. Straight into detail. Mining for the real ore of her.

"Do I know her?" I asked.

"No," he said. But I didn't believe him.

"Does she know about me?" I asked him.

"Yes," he said. But what would he have told her? Not the dear things. Not the big things. He wouldn't have told her about the time, after my operation, when I lay in the hospital bed in Bangor and he sat there all day long with his laptop and book, just being there in the room with me so that, whenever I rolled out of the fog of my opiated stupor, he was right there, with his familiar shirt on, with his laptop, sitting in the hospital chair.

You're still here, I said. I didn't know what time it was. Time had gotten all blurry and strange and stretched out by the drugs and the pain in between the drugs.

Of course, he told me, looking up. *Where else would I be?* he asked me. And I knew he would always be there, right there in the room with me.

Did Natalie know about that?

Did Natalie know about the time that my father got the diagnosis and my mother and I sat in the doctor's office with him and heard the news? And how my dad leaned forward with his head cocked to one side so he could hear better, and my mother was sitting there beside him with her hands in her lap and all I could think was of how long they'd been together and how permanent they'd always seemed to me. And later, when I went out to the parking lot to get the car and drove up to the hospital entrance to pick them up, how small they both looked, standing there—my mother who had always been so tall. *We'll do whatever we can to help him get better,* the doctor had told us, *but you have to understand that we might fail.*

And did Natalie know, because how could she know, if David hadn't told her, how I had driven them back to their house and got them settled, and then gone home? I'd have to tell the kids, but not yet, not yet. Did she know how I had managed to go into the house and make the supper, and chat with my daughter, and how, later on, when David had finally arrived and I had told the children in a light voice, *We're going out for a walk. We'll be back in half an hour*—how then, finally, only then, when we were a few blocks from the house in the cold night in the abandoned wintertime town, how then I turned to him and pushed my face into his chest cold with the cold night air and how I had cried and cried and cried and, later in the night lying awake, unable to sleep, turned to him crying and crying for my father? Did Natalie know about that?

Did Natalie know about the silly giggles we got making up stories about people we knew? *Good Ole Yankee Ear Wax* and the *Secret Lives of the Neighbors.* Hoarse with no sleep, lying in the bed, giggling helplessly.

Did Natalie know about the time last summer when we were having lamb chops he'd cooked on the grill and red wine from Argentina with my friend Rita from Arizona and she was trying to describe the kind of wild animals they have there—the wild boars and how they were *dog pigs,* she kept insisting. *Pig dogs.* And how all three of us started laughing and how David had turned to me in the midst of all that and had said, *Oh, Virginia, I love you.*

Did Natalie know that? What version of our relationship had she been given? That I was cold and too busy for him? That I was too distant? That I didn't care? Maybe Natalie had been told that the spark had gone out of our relationship. What are the things that men tell women they are pursuing? When they already have someone else?

So now I asked David, "What does Natalie know about me?"

But he didn't answer.

"How could she do that?" I asked him. Angry now at the

mythical, invisible Natalie with her smallish breasts and her brown, longish hair and her stupid, multisyllabic movie star name. "I would never do that to another woman."

Later, thinking over and over this scene obsessively, I was struck by how stupid that sounded. *So what?* So what if you wouldn't do something? Does that mean nobody else would? Obviously not. What did I think? That good moral behavior was a kind of kitty—a pool of some sort—and, if you threw in your share of good behavior, you got to divide the good behavior spoils—that you benefited from it? At fifty I still thought that?

How stupid I was, I kept thinking later. How stupid to believe him. How stupid to trust him. How stupid to take for granted his enormous love based on such silly, flimsy reasoning—that he had been with me for ten years. That we had shared so much. That I still desired him. That he seemed to be the one in my life—the one man who would last.

How stupid, and how shortsighted, and how terrible to be at the end of it now.

He didn't answer me when I said something about never doing that to another woman. Maybe he nodded a little as if agreeing with me. *No, you wouldn't do that.* But I had seen what was under the scrim of his anguish, his mask of sorrow and regret. I'd seen his fury with me.

Maybe it *was* all my fault.

But that would come later. Now it was only shock and the firelight. Only his sad face, the corners of his mouth pulled down in an exaggerated frown. It must hurt his facial muscles, I thought, frowning like that.

There was one small sane part of my mind, like a little animal, rummaging around in the tossed-open drawers of my confusion. There must be things I should say now. There must be questions I wanted answers to. Now was the time. It was New Year's Eve. He had just told me this news. I was at a certain advantage that I would never recapture. In negotiation, timing is everything. I just wished I were up to the task—that I could think of all the things I ought to say.

But I was so stunned. I was speaking through a thick sort of blankety feeling, that covered everything, that made it impossible to think.

"What did you think would happen?"

He shrugged. "I didn't know."

"Did you bring her to your house?"

He hesitated. Then he answered. "Yes."

"Do Beth and Parker know?"

Again the hesitation.

Then, "No. They don't know."

But I thought they probably did. I thought that probably they knew all about it. That was why they hadn't answered my e-mail; they had known this was coming. They knew he was going to tell me tonight, on New Year's Eve. That seemed like the worst of it—that he had chosen this night to tell me, but it turned out, I found out later, in conversation with other wounded birds, that holidays are popular times for such revelations.

Months later, sitting at lunch with a bunch of women friends.

He told me on New Year's Eve, I said, trying to make it sound funny.

Oh, yeah. Well, mine told me on my birthday, said Sora.

You're kidding me. But listen to this: I know somebody whose boyfriend broke up with her on Valentine's Day.

But somehow New Year's Eve seemed to me to be the worst. Because it was so freighted with meaning—dense with expectation. His act a dark smudge across the year to come. Because it was the beginning of everything and then it was also the end. Because that was when it happened to me.

"You brought her to your house?"

"Yes."

I shook my head. Thought of how, early in our relationship, I used to go there unexpectedly, pop in.

One time in a Halloween mask, about nine o'clock, going out late in the cold, bright air, I'd gotten into my car and driven all the way up the dark roads through Sinclair, lit up and heavily policed for the night, with toilet paper in the trees blowing its ghostly streamers in a wild dance; drove the rest of the way, the long road uphill and down, and glided into his driveway. Parked quietly, slipped out of the car, put on my big wild rubbery mask, crept into the house, ran across the kitchen and into his study. *Aha!* I yelled and he had jumped, startled, and began to laugh.

Virginia, shaking his head at me. *Oh, Virginia. You're something else.*

And what if I'd turned up one of those nights—I assumed they were nights—when Natalie was there at his house? Turned up in a Halloween mask. Turned up with a little table to present to him. Turned up in tears as I had the time my daughter came home from college with a tattoo. Turned up on a cold spring afternoon as I used to, and David would come to the door and say, *Come in. Let me get you something. Have you eaten?*

It seemed like a long time since I had turned up at his house.

And now, sitting here with him, it was my last chance to ask him things. Which I was botching. Because I was so confused and so in shock and everything was in slow motion. I tried to think of something I should be saying and all I could think of was, "God, it must have been weird, knowing you were coming down to tell me this tonight. It must have been so weird for you in the movie store looking at movies. *What Women Want. Moonstruck. Torch Song Trilogy.* Sort of like *you* were in a movie. Woody Allen or something."

He actually laughed at that. "Oh, Virginia, that's why I love you."

I thought, for a second: Good. Then this is all over? All this nonsense about leaving me?

But then he added, "And that's why this is so hard."

And I still didn't get it. Somehow, because I was asking these questions about Natalie, because I was needling him a little and still managing to crack jokes, I thought I might charm him back. We were both still standing on this side of something together, observing the world. Him with his arm around me. Making jokes at others' expense. Making rude comments. Right now, before anything else happened, before we turned any more pages, right now we were still in this chapter. That's why I could ask these questions. Because we were the ones who were together—Dave and Virginia—and *she* was the interloper in our own small, private garden.

But—*that's why this is so hard.*

What's so hard? I wanted to say. *Telling me this? Hard for you? It's hard for me, you lummox!* But I still didn't believe it. Because this was who we were. This was who I was. Half him.

"Are you breaking up with me?" I asked him. And even as I was asking, I knew how dumb it sounded.

Duh.

Of course he was breaking up with me. That's what this was about. That's why he was telling me this. That's why he was crying. That's why he was looking at me in this sorry way like he was the sad banker—*hate to do it*—foreclosing on a loan. Like he was a rueful and despondent parent. *It's for your own good, honey.* Like he was a teacher giving me the bad grade so I'd learn from this. Like he was in charge. Like he got to be the one who decided this. I was supposed to be the one to leave him—if he didn't straighten out. If something better came along. If I had the nerve.

But I had always chosen him. Again and again. In spite of everything. The boredom, his depression, the lack of sex in the last few months, the times when he was irritable and unpleasant. I had chosen him. I had chosen to stay with him. Thinking it was wrong to leave him now, when it would hurt him so much.

"You'll be fine," he told me.

How did he know what I'd be?

He was my man. He was, finally, the man that I trusted and loved. He was the man—imperfect and cumbersome and awkward though he was, that made my world whole. He was the man who knew me. He was the man who understood how ignorant I was, how shallow I could be, how silly and demanding and selfish and stupid and darling I could be—and who loved me anyway.

And now, looking into his ruined face, his mouth turned down, eyes sad and full of his regretful tears, I wanted to say something. But I was stuck in a gluey slowness, a gummy strangeness, a bad, dreamy feeling. I could no longer move. I had nothing to say. I couldn't find the one magical thing that would bring him back to me. That would cut through the gum. That would cut through the thick air of the room between us. That would be clear and sharp and perfect in the dark, imperfect night.

I tried to talk. I told him I didn't know what to say. I told him I never thought he would do this. That he could have done this. I wasn't really sad yet. I was just in this numb dimness.

The room itself seemed dim now, like it was full of smoke or something. I was supposed to be the great negotiator; I thought in that part of my mind that darted around looking through the drawers, looking for some talisman, some magic charm that would keep him.

He liked it when I was funny. I tried to think of a joke. *Ever heard the one about the old man who goes to heaven? How about the two old married people who go to the sex counselor? What's the difference between a pit bull and a premenstrual woman?*

Suddenly I thought of Brad, a man I went out with for a while when I was in college. He was tall and strange and lived in an air stream trailer outside of town. He was great in bed, had an enormous penis. Surprising, that penis of his, because he was so thin. We had sex a lot that spring in the silver trailer. He had long messy hair and his clothes looked too big for him—ill-fitting scarecrow clothes. My friends all thought he was weird and couldn't figure out what I saw in him. I thought he was probably brilliant, that he would be famous one day for something. There was something about him. I didn't love him exactly, but I enjoyed him. He was so odd.

My best friend, Ming, said, "Look, this guy is too weird. Just dump him. Tell him it's not working out."

Together we rehearsed what I would say to him.

"Take him someplace neutral," Ming advised. "You know, out to coffee or something."

"We don't go out to coffee," I told her.

Mostly I saw him at his trailer. I'd be walking along the side-walk and he'd drive up in his beat-up old Saab, roll down the window, say, "You comin' or what?"

He was from a rich family, though he liked to act poor. He knew about skiing and horses and boats. He was more than he was. But Ming was right, he was weird.

So one day I wound up riding my bike out to his trailer. He was all wrong for me. When I was with him, I felt removed from the world. And what good was that? I wanted to be right inside the world—where everything happened.

I sort of hoped he wasn't there, but his car was parked in the little dusty place next to the dull silver side of the trailer. I leaned my bike up against a tree and knocked on the door, which was curved, I remembered. I remembered thinking how much I liked that little trailer, how cool it was that he had rented it for the semester. How cool he was, in fact, in a haphazard, almost homeless way.

He was so tall he had to hunch over to open the door for me.

"Come on in," he said, and bustled back toward the kitchen area where he was making lunch. Nobody I knew made lunch. They all just went to the Caf. But here he had lettuce set out on the tiny counter and a loaf of bread and the square little icebox stood open and inside I could see his tidy bachelor food: a car-ton of milk, some carrots, yellow cheese.

I stood there, awkwardly, near the door.

"Wanna sit down? Wanna sandwich?" he asked me over his

shoulder. "Or did you come here for something else?" waggling his eyebrows at me like Groucho Marx. This usually made me laugh.

I had rehearsed it—what I would say—why was it so hard?

"Brad," I said at last.

"Yeeeeeessss?"

"I think we need to stop seeing each other," I told him.

He kept spreading mustard on his bread. Didn't turn around.

"Did you hear me, Brad?"

"Yeah. You want some cheese?"

He held a piece of cheese out on a knife. I laughed and took it. It was almost enough—that gesture of the cheese—to win me back.

So now I thought if I could just think up some quirky funny stunt like that to pull with David, then he wouldn't leave me. He would retract his statement. He would not have had an affair. He wouldn't even know anyone named Natalie. He wouldn't mean all that stuff he'd said about being unhappy and angry with me. He'd just be the way he always was. And he'd laugh that laugh he laughed when he was pleased with me. When he said I was darling and impossible. When he said that no one had ever made him laugh as much as I did. That's what he'd say now. If I could just think up the right line.

But I couldn't think. I could only stare at him. I didn't think I'd looked at him this much in years. My mouth was open, so I shut it, and tears were coming down my face but I didn't wipe them away because there were more and more. What was the use?

What was the use of anything? Of clever phrases. Funny tales. Of tears or Kleenex. It was all decided. You could turn or not turn the page. You could stop reading the story. But you knew—you couldn't make yourself not know—that buried in the next chapter was the sad part that you didn't want to read.

I didn't know what to say, so I said, "I've got this food, you want some?"

And so, in a sort of rueful parody of a New Year's celebration, the two of us trooped into my kitchen and I took out the special cheese, brought forth the bread and the two champagne flutes and the olives that were so dark and smooth and perfectly shiny in the red bowl I'd picked especially for this occasion.

"Will you open the champagne?" I asked him, because he was the man.

It was very good champagne. I'd been saving it.

"I'll put some more wood on the fire," I told him, carrying the tray into the living room.

"Do you want me to do that?" he asked in a polite way.

"No, that's okay," I said, and I was surprised at how normal I sounded.

I took the screen away from the fire, careful not to get my hands all sooty. What does it matter—sooty? I thought, and almost slid back into that tearful catatonic state, but then grabbed hold of myself, took a stick of wood, put it into the fire, and the sparks flew up. It was warm on my face, the way the sun would feel warm, if it were summer.

He came in, and handed me a glass of champagne.

"I don't think we make a toast at this point, do you?" I asked him with a crooked little smile which even, broken as it was, I hoped was charming.

I wanted to charm him. With the champagne, with my valor, with my quirkiness. With the cheese.

But the champagne tasted terrible. Fizzy and sour.

"Is there something wrong with this?" I asked him.

"I don't think so," he told me.

What did he know? Nothing tasted right. I tried the cheese, but it just felt like a big thing lodged in my mouth. Bread? No.

I couldn't eat, it turned out.

But I ought to eat. Eat something. He was eating. I saw him munching away on his bread and cheese, drinking a nice drink of his champagne. He was feeling better, I observed. The hard part for him was over. He'd told me. He was like the kid who has the terrible fall and is all shaken up but then gets bandaged and has a good cry and is sitting at the table with something good to eat and a story to look forward to—all cozy again. He'd been worrying about this for weeks. For months. Now it was over.

But not for me. I tried to put the bread in my mouth but had to take it out because I was crying again.

"Who will I talk to?" I asked him. All bravado gone. I hated how I sounded, but I couldn't help it.

"Nick. You can talk to Nick," he told me. "You can talk to Rose."

But he was the one I went to. He was the one I told.

"Who will you talk to? Natalie?" I said her name like it was a dirty thing.

He looked at me, stopped eating his bread and cheese.

"I may talk to her," he said evenly. "And I've been seeing a therapist."

Since when? I'd been asking him to see someone for years and he always put me off. *I don't like talking to those guys,* he always told me. *I don't know who to go to,* he always said.

I had gotten him the names of several people—men and women—he could talk to. I had gotten their phone numbers for him. I had offered to call for him, to set up the appointment. He always put me off. *No, it's okay. I'll do it myself,* he said. But he never did.

Only now, it turned out, he did do it.

"What?"

"I've been seeing someone—regularly—for the past two years."

Two years? What else? What else didn't I know? Did he have another family somewhere? Was he one of those guys with a secret life? Had he had lovers all along? All this time?

That's when it began—the racing back through the events, the tearing apart of the drawers. The obsessive remembering of the months. The dates and places. Times and phone calls. How he sounded on different days. Where he might have been. What he said. What he told me. What he didn't say.

I remembered one morning at breakfast when he mentioned something about his sit-ups.

I didn't know you did sit-ups, I said. *When do you do them?* I asked in a teasing way.

But he was completely serious. *Every day,* he said. He sounded stern, almost angry. *Every day.* Then, *There are a lot of things you don't know about me, Virginia.*

Evidently.

"What does he think of—of what you've been doing? Your therapist? Did you talk to him about it?"

"Yes. And I've talked to my minister."

"You have?"

Then I wanted to know again. "Do Beth and Parker know? Does Sarah know?"

"No."

But I didn't believe him.

"What did they say?"

"Shouldn't you eat something?" he asked. He was still munching away. He looked almost contented.

I looked at the bread and cheese in my hand. I looked at the sour champagne in the flute. "Yeah," I said, but I couldn't.

"What did they say to do?"

"My therapist told me we should each make a list of what we needed from the relationship."

"A list?"

This was the sort of thing we would normally laugh about. The sort of thing we made fun of: couples therapy. Couples making lists.

"What did the minister say?"

"He said I should tell you. They both said that, that I should tell you."

Then I just sat there. I couldn't think of anything else I was supposed to say. The fire was there. The Christmas tree full of ornaments, full of its little lights. *It'll be nice,* I'd said to him. *The tree's still up.* The champagne in its dark green bottle. The cold night outside. The black windows.

I started crying again. Not hard, this time. Not the way I'd cry later. Just a slow leaking out of my tears.

"Should I go?" he asked me.

"No," I said.

So we sat there. He would give me this. A little more time on the green couch to absorb what he'd told me. But I couldn't think of anything to say and finally, about ten, I said to him, "You should go."

"Are you sure?" but he sounded relieved.

He could go out into the cold bright clean night air. He could leave this house full of tears and green couches. Full of firelight and Christmas lights and my sad, reproachful face. He could go out and get into his Jeep and, if he was cautious, he could keep from skipping as he went, as he might want to, as he went down the driveway toward his dark truck, which would gleam, the smooth flanks of it, in the far, cold light of the moon.

•••

He got up, and I got up, too, and I picked up the tray full of food I couldn't eat, and he took the bottle, companionably, back into the kitchen for me. We had done this a thousand times. After an evening with friends, cleaning up together, he at the sink, me putting food in Saran Wrap. We had discussed bits and pieces from the evening's conversation. We had cleaned up after a night alone together. Watching a movie, reading on the couch, playing a game of cribbage by the fire. We had left the kitchen clean and orderly, gone up together to my room and we had lain down together and made love or we had not made love. We had talked in the dark room.

Now he started to put things away. He knew my little systems. But I said, "I can do that." I didn't want him to open the refrigerator door.

I didn't want him rooting around in my possessions. Looking at my plates in the cupboard. Putting his hands in the sink. I wanted him gone.

But then, when he took his coat out of the closet, when he put it on, it seemed so final. That he really was leaving me.

I walked him toward the door and then, when we were near it, he turned and he put his arms around me. Put his face against my hair.

"Good-bye," he told me.

"This isn't the New Year's Eve I imagined," he said to me.

"But this is the one you made."

"Yes. This is the one I made."

We sounded, I thought, as if our words had been rehearsed.

He opened the door and the cold air came in around him. Turned once, looked at me with a sad face. Went out.

I watched him walk down the steps and across the driveway toward his truck. I thought he might skip, after all, but he walked somberly, quietly, and in a dignified way.

I saw him get into his Jeep and then I switched off the porch light, just as he turned on his headlights, illuminating my house and the dark and silent doorway where I stood.

13

Finally, about 3 A.M., I took a sleeping pill and fell into a pale, thin sleep. The wind continued to howl around the house. I dreamt or I didn't dream. Later I couldn't remember if I had slept at all.

I was awake at dawn; remembered right away what happened the night before. I lay in the bed without moving—heavy and still.

I talked to myself the way I would talk to a child in a dark car after a serious accident. *Okay. You need to get up. It's New Year's Day. You can change the calendar. It's 2003. You can make a list of things to do this year. It's going to be okay. You don't know what's going to happen. We don't know. It's okay. You're just here. The kids are fine. You're healthy. You have both your legs. You can still walk.*

And so I tottered into the new year.

Down to the kitchen. Open the calendar. Look at the January picture for signs and omens. It was a Japanese art calendar. I get one every year, and open each month with great ritual. Bamboo trees in twilight. Rains of autumn. The mysterious tiny faraway bridges. This time a wild sea. Fitting, I thought. The dark turquoise waters tossed with their whitecaps. Whirlpools at Naruto.

I could feel, right under the surface of these ordinary, comforting details of my morning, the grim hard place of my pain. I wanted to define it but I didn't want to touch it. It was like a big bad smell in the room—my emotion. It was like a terrible accident I'd been forced to witness. *Don't look!* somebody warning me, but I had to look—the dark bright blood, the mangled limbs, the bright white shock of the bone.

But here were the familiar things of my life: the golden light in the kitchen. The tall old-fashioned cabinets. *Oh, I love your kitchen.* The blue mug with my coffee and milk. The black windows that would lighten soon. The flower in the blue glass vase. The two rocks Rita gave me, one black, one white. The iron leaf Jeff made. The little china statue my father brought me from a trip to France. The photograph of my son and daughter. The calendar. Whirlpools at Naruto. That wild sea.

Okay, I said to myself. *Okay okay.* The slightly hypnotic tone. *Okay okay you're okay now.* The way you would coax an animal out of hiding—shivering, scared. *It's okay.*

And under the surface the hard fact of my own disappearance. Like a cheap couch—the big bolstery comfy cushiony hugeness of it but right underneath the hard arm, the hard bone of the frame. Putting your head down: *Ow. It's hard right under there.*

This was how it was. It started that morning. It started the night before. It went on and on, this feeling of disorientation. Someone had stolen my life. With a part of myself I was watching. From somewhere. Who was I? What was I without him? I was only a ghost of myself.

"I can't stop thinking," I would tell everyone. All stops out—pride abandoned. I told everyone in those first few weeks about it.

"You don't have to talk about it if you don't want to," said my friend Denise.

But I brushed that aside.

"I have to tell you what happened." As if it were even interesting.

It wasn't interesting. Another thing I thought about lying in the bed at night trying to sleep. It was too hot. I pushed the covers away to feel the cold night air. The heat from my overcharged body. I shoved the comforter off. It was no comfort. And thought, this is not interesting. This was not an interesting story I was living. This was the most ordinary of stories. I'd heard it a million times. *He left her. He dumped her. He found someone else.*

I tasted the various ways to tell it—with the jaunty tone: *Oh yeah, we're through.* Tried: *It's for the best.* Tried: *Look, he's an asshole.* Tried serious, somberly, but bravely: *It's been kind of hard.* The downward look, the hesitation, the enormous understatement: *It's been a little rough.*

How to position it? How to market my heartbreak? How to tell everybody what happened? Not just my friends. But everyone. Didn't I have to tell everyone? Or did everyone already know? The girls in the shop where I got my newspaper. The man at the deli counter in the supermarket, cutting his weary provolone, slicing his honeyed ham. He knew something was up, didn't he?

"Have a good holiday?" he asked me two days later. Had he no mercy? Had he no sense of timing? Of irony? For a moment I was torn—wanted to burst into hot tears right there. Tell him everything. Standing there with my aimless shopping cart. The bread. The bananas. Should get some oranges. Need fruit in winter. The skim milk. Calcium: very important. The hothouse tomatoes with their fragrant, spicy leaves. All of it tumbled in the cart before me.

Just give me my cheese, I wanted to say to him. *Just hand over the cheddar. Slide me a slab of fontina. Shave off some corned beef.* But shouldn't I also tell him? Shouldn't I? He was a nice man. I had often observed his wrists. Used to think he was kind of handsome, back in those faraway days when I had a boyfriend and could look at other men and consider them, imagine them, and reject them. Flirt the way women flirt, knowing nothing would come of it. The understood polite shimmer of interest but—*Oh, I see you've got a ring. You have someone. Well, me too. We're both taken, but aren't we both still—at our age—still, in a certain way, attractive, and see how here, even in Maine, even in the deep of winter, we acknowledge it?* He had nice wrists. He had nice hands cutting the deli products. Lifting the heavy pastramis from their cool case. He had a lovely face.

He was staring at me. "What can I do for you today?" he asked in his too-hearty voice. Did I look strange? But the strangest part was, I was sure I didn't.

•••

But that came later. Now it was only morning. I was at my desk and I was faced with the task that normally delighted me—writing a list of things to do in the new year.

If he'd been there with me—if all that hadn't happened—he would have lain in bed a little longer, after I went downstairs. He would have stayed in the bed, lying on his back perhaps, turning to lie on his side. He might have fallen back to sleep or he might have gotten up and taken his slippers out of the closet, slid his feet into them, found his robe, which he kept there. He might have been wearing those dark red pajamas I gave him for Christmas. Might not have said all that confusing stuff about them being wet. He might have come down finally, quietly, gone into the kitchen, taken the yellow mug, which was the mug for David, out of the cupboard, poured himself a cup of coffee or made himself a cup of green tea. Sat in the chair in the window, looked out at the coming morning—the band of pink across the sky, the quiet yard. My car in the drive. His truck nosed in behind. The frost on the windshield. The black, sharp twigs of winter trees against the sky.

That's how it might have been. But now, as I take up the bright white large index cards it all just seems like an endless toil. What I will do. What I might do. What I hope to do. All of it alone. All of it without him in my life.

I have been thinking all this while standing in his bedroom staring down unseeing at his bed. It's dark in the room. I know I have to leave. But there is something I am searching for that I still haven't found. Something I want to recover from his house. What is it?

I remember how, early in our relationship, a year or two into it, he went away for the long hiking trip on the Appalachian Trail he'd planned years ago with his daughter. The night before he left, I stayed with him at his house. We made love as if we were drowning. It was summer and the windows were open. The room felt light and like a caravan. The next day he left, early, and after I had driven him over to their meeting place in Millinocket, I came back to his house, aimless with grief. Three whole months without him! What would I do with myself?

I was exhausted. We had stayed up most of the night making love, holding each other, and talking. I had been unable to sleep. Now I was tired and it was hot out, the sky bright and hard and the back field silver with heat. I went through the rooms of his house that hot afternoon all alone.

I went up to his bedroom and stood like this, right by the bed. That was almost ten years ago, that I had stood here that day—that different girl that I was. I stood by the bed and looked down at it. I was exhausted, tired the way I feel tired now. And I lay down on the bed and I put my face against his pillow and I smelled the smell of him and I felt as if he might, at any moment, come into the room and be there again.

So now I lie down on the bed the way I did on that long-ago day. The comforter cover is cool and unfamiliar after all this time. Was it always this rough? I pull it back a little so that I can put my face against his pillow. I lie there on my side and I can smell his smell and it is familiar and this feels more real than anything that has happened all year.

He might come in at any moment. It wouldn't be so great, if he were to come in and find me here. I probably ought to get up and leave, while I still can. Go out into the night; get back to my car in Sinclair still parked in the lot by Rogerson's, the windshield shining like licorice—a dark and lonely lozenge in the night.

But I can't get up quite yet. I need to lie here. I have been tired, so tired, for so long.

It was cold; the first cold day of what would become one of the coldest Januaries on record. So cold, as everyone kept saying over and over saying and saying all month long and then, looking backward, long into the spring and summer still talking about it—so cold it took your breath away. And it did. My breath, if I had any, was snatched out of my mouth, grabbed out of my throat by the cold. *Whup!*

I was dressed for anything. What was I wearing? Warm clothes. A hodgepodge. I had pulled my warmest polar fleece sweatshirt, warmest socks, warmest pants, warmest jacket, scarf, hat, my double mittens over my pajamas like a crazy woman.

No one can tell, I muttered to myself. No one could tell if I was dressed or not dressed, if I was crazy or not crazy. There would be no one anywhere—on the road, on the path leading up into the woods, in the garden tucked away behind its stone walls with its beautiful view. *What a beautiful view!* Everything.

Everything we did together. All those years. Everything was marked with him now. It all belonged to him—my whole life. The garden where we went together. The door of my house. The front seat of my car. It was all his. Nothing was mine anymore. I had thought I was saving it for myself, but I had given it all away.

The car started hard. It was so cold. Too cold to take my mittens off, to fuck with the key in the lock, to adjust any of the knobs in the car, to turn off the radio, which was blaring some falsely jolly Top 100 Countdown against my will. All the songs I had listened to all year. The music just noise to me now. Oh, this is so boring, I thought. Was this how it was going to be? It was 7 A.M. Even the sky was brittle with the cold. Hardly any snow. A dry scattering, a thin layer over the frozen brown leaves of last fall.

14

I climbed the big stone steps up the side of the hill where the garden sat carved into the rock. I have gone there so often, for so many years; I know every turn in the path, every step in the stairs.

I took the path that led over the rocks. In a few days it would be impassible with the inevitable ice of January, but December had been gentle, and the trail was still clear.

At the top, a little stone chapel overlooks the town. There is a perfect long view of the river and the place where it bends into the ocean far below. There was no one else on the whole hill. And no one for miles around.

I went into the small building and sat down on one of the little wooden benches that lined the sides. Initials carved into the wood. Some old, some newer. Jagged hearts and old, lost names.

One day the previous August, when I had climbed up there through the hot hum of the summer afternoon, I had come upon a fat young couple in there making out. As I approached I couldn't see at first it was two people—it just looked like one big shape on the floor. Eyes dazzled with the bright afternoon sun, I was almost at the doorway before I recognized the angle of the bodies, the motion of the boy as he rocked into the girl beneath him. They had spread their jackets on the floor and the large boy was on top of the large girl. True Mainers, from Bangor or Downeast. The boy dressed in blue jeans and the girl in a tight yellow stretch top. They had their clothes on, or most of them—the girl's shirt was pulled up and the boy had his hands on her. The girl's hands tight around his back, clutching his shirt.

The girl saw me first, over his shoulder.

Her eyes, ringed with black o's of makeup, widened.

"Roy!" the girl whispered—as if his name were a secret that I couldn't hear, as if maybe I hadn't noticed them yet, though right away I turned, with what was meant to be a kindly chuckle— an oh-I-was-young-once-myself kind of chuckle—and stood outside with my back to them so they could straighten their clothes, get up, go out, or go stand at the far side of the little chapel and gaze out at the scenery as if that's what they'd been doing all along.

"Roy! Somebody's here!"

The boy grunted, rolled off. I could hear his body hit the stone floor, and I heard him mumble something, but I couldn't tell what he was saying, and I suddenly felt not chuckly or kind at all, but sort of desperate and sad.

I thought of heading back right away down the steep trail which I had just ascended. But I had so longed for the cool interior stone. I'd been thinking about it all day.

Finally, the two kids dodged out past me, hesitant, too big, and embarrassed; carrying their jackets in their hands, not looking back, and made their awkward descent down the rocky path.

But the chapel smelled weird after they left and not the way it usually did—cool and mossy, dim and still. I wanted to feel tranquil, but I did not feel tranquil. The small room was full of their teenage sexuality. The walls imprinted with their awkward lust. I didn't stay long that day, and it was a week or more before I went back up.

But no one would be there on this New Year's Day.

The chapel stood wide open. There was no door. No windows. Just open spaces where the light and air came in. In winter sometimes snow blew in during a storm and heaped up on the benches and the floor in perfect piles, but there was no snow yet.

The place felt abandoned, colder than it was, the sky outside the dead white bright forgetful sky of winter.

I didn't want to sit down on the cold wood bench, lean back against the colder hard stone wall. I walked to the far end and looked out at the view.

All the way up I had thought and not thought of what happened. I had concentrated on the climb, with fierce attention to my legs and my arms; the cold still air. Now here I was and there was nothing to do. Nothing left to climb. I thought I'd pray or say something or find something up here the way I sometimes had. One time a bunch of flowers. Another time, standing upright on a rock, an entire unopened package of Wild Cherry LifeSavers. There were no such prizes here today. Only my own sharp breathing and the blank, pale, early morning sky.

I stood at the open doorway looking out. The river far below looked still and almost sullen. The little village where I live, with its trees and houses and one white, tall church, looked like a toy town. I couldn't see my house, but I knew where it was, beyond a certain line of trees, just down from where the Quimbys' long white house dominated the far field. The pasture that stretched out beyond. The little cemetery tucked in there. The view was the same as it had always been. Everything miniature and far away. How would I inhabit those roads and pastures when I went back down?

That was what I had to piece together, over the next long weeks: patch together a random gaggle of friends and family to fill the intimate space that David had left vacant in my life. I did have close friends, wonderful friends. There was Nick, who had been my friend for years and years. We'd seen each other through bad marriages and worse affairs. We'd comforted one another through lonely New Year's Eves, unattended birthdays, unintended consequences of lousy marriages. He could be counted on to show up at my door, as he did, that first day, to sit on the couch and listen to my story, to help me be unashamed of crying, to follow up each day after with a phone call at some odd hour: *Just checking in to see how you're doing,* in his kind voice. He was a psychologist. He was very organized. No doubt he had a neat list somewhere of both friends and clients whom he called each day and then gradually tapered off to once a week when they appeared to be doing better. He mattered greatly to me and his kindness mattered. He could be counted on to hug me when I needed hugging, to listen to my stories again and again, listen to me repeat the same things over and over. Endlessly *there for me* as they say. It helped.

And my other friends helped, too. Marie, who was far away but always nearby on the phone. Who sent me a bouquet of all white flowers and a note *I love you* when she heard the news.

Mary D. and Rose and Susan. They all rallied round. My parents, in Florida, befuddled by the news, and given only half the story, sent "their best" in e-mails and occasional phone calls in which my mother suggested a trip to *Italy, sweetie, it would do you good. Go with one of your friends. Go with Rose or Susan. Or maybe you and Judy could go.*

They understood, or thought they understood, what I was going through. They cared about me. They wanted me to feel better. But they wanted me to feel better sooner than I did. I wanted to feel better, too. But I was surprised at how it hung on, the sad feeling, the anger and the desperation.

It wasn't as if he'd died, I told myself, but in a way it was worse. At least if he'd died there'd be some dignity in my grief. As it was, all the lies he had told me made our whole relationship feel false. What was real? What had been true? Our history was like a house that I kept walking through, not knowing which floorboards were rotten, where I might fall through.

It was, as everyone kept saying, a particularly cold winter. It never got over ten degrees, the whole month of January, when I was still reeling with the sudden slug to the chest. I had my job, thank God. That was what I would concentrate on.

I woke up every morning *bang!* in my bed, if I had slept at all. Usually I did manage to sleep toward morning, when the night-time thoughts passed off and I finally drifted downward into sleep. I woke up to windows etched with white peacock feathers of frost. Outside the sky a far and distant color. Sometimes pale blue and streaked with pink. Sometimes too cold to tell.

It didn't snow much that January. There was nothing to soften the sharp, hard rocks of winter. Nothing to lighten the landscape, curtain the view, to make the angle of the branches less abrupt and sharp against the sky.

I did the things I thought I ought to do. The things I knew would eventually somehow pay off. I got up early. I went to my desk. I wrote in my journal (*I hate him I hate him I miss him I miss him yesterday I tried to eat but I can't eat. I hate everything.*) My journal was the one place I allowed myself this kind of maudlin enterprise—the mining of my deepest rage and pain. The one place I could dump it. I knew I couldn't dump it forever on my friends. They would tire of my sorrow the way I had tired, other times, of theirs. The husband who left and kept leaving—how often I'd heard that sad scene of his leaving! *And then he said to me. And then he picked up his bag. And then he went upstairs and got his jacket out of the hall closet. That was what really got me, when he got his jacket out of the hall closet.* I resisted, had resisted for years, the temptation to mouth the words along with Corinne. *That was what really got me, when he got his jacket out of the hall closet.*

Sometimes I thought my own enormous, unexpected sorrow was a penance for all the times I had dismissed my friends' deep pain. I thought I was being a good, kind friend, listening to it, helping them through it, taking them on walks or out to supper to dine on their desperation and to cheer them up. But hadn't I always held back a bit? Hadn't there always been a little bored deep core of me, a little smug ignoble center where I'd thought: Well, if she'd fixed her hair up. If she'd lost a little weight. If she hadn't nagged him, if she'd gone on that trip with him he always wanted to go on, if she'd . . . Or, alternately: Well, how great was he anyway? She was always complaining about him. The way he cut his eggs with a knife and fork—the sound it made. It used to drive her crazy. She would tell me. God! I can hear him from all the way upstairs, she would say. So wasn't she glad to be rid of him? And wasn't he always kind of boring? Kind of pompous? Kind of this or that?

Wasn't he always kind of . . .

But now all those mean questions seemed just that—mean. Because all of that might be true, I realized, but none of that matters in the face of pain.

15

"I don't think you're depressed," my therapist told me. I hadn't seen her in over a year—but had called after the breakup to make an appointment. Now I was sitting in her little office with the dove gray walls. I was sitting on the two-person couch where often couples sit. Maybe I should have brought David here, back when I had a chance. Maybe we should have had couples' counseling. But we'd always made fun of couples who had counseling, of couples who were trying to work on their relationship. *If you have to work on it,* we said to one another. *If you have to work on it . . .*

But you did have to work on it, it turns out, and I hadn't.

"It really caught you by surprise, didn't it?" my therapist asked.

"It was out of the blue."

"I didn't expect it," I said.

I wanted her to explain what was happening to me. How I was. I felt as if a little engine inside of my body was running in high gear. Running and buzzing like crazy. The accelerator was stuck and it was using up all of my energy, keeping me awake. It would never let up. I couldn't stop it; I didn't think I could stand it.

It had been a month since the split.

"I can't eat hardly anything," I told my therapist. "I'm trying.

I'm trying to get exercise so I'll be hungry but I can't eat. I can't sleep. I just lie there. I took Tylenol PM a couple of times, but I don't want to take too much. I don't want to get addicted."

"I don't think you're going to get addicted."

"I can't sleep."

"I think it's okay to take the Tylenol. I think it's good to get the exercise. Are you eating anything at all?"

She didn't look alarmed. She never looked alarmed. She wasn't worried that I'd dropped ten pounds in three weeks. That I couldn't sleep more than a couple of hours at a time. That I had these dark dangerous circles under my eyes. She didn't seem worried so now maybe I wouldn't be, either.

"Sometimes."

She looked at me in a kind and interested way.

"Sometimes?"

"Yeah. I can eat if I'm with someone. Like I had to go to lunch with some people from work, and then I could eat. Not a lot. But it didn't scare me the way it does when I'm by myself."

"Scare you?"

"Well, that's not it, exactly. I just hate the thought of eating anything. Putting anything into my stomach. Especially certain things. Dark foods."

"What do you mean, 'dark foods'?"

"Like chocolate. I used to love chocolate. I can't eat it anymore. Not since what happened. And I can't eat meat or anything sort of spicy or tomatoey or dark red. I can't imagine eating it and even the things I do eat seem to turn dark when they get inside me. I don't like how I feel after I eat. Coffee's dark. And normally I love coffee. Any kind of meat, though. Especially."

"What seems okay to you?" She asked me as if she really cared, and I was grateful for her simulated concern. That's what I was paying her for, after all.

But shouldn't we be talking about more substantive things? Didn't she get how bad it was? How crazy I felt? What did I have to say to get her to notice? We're not just fooling around here. I might even kill myself! Shouldn't we be preventing my possible suicide? But I should keep that part a secret, at least for now. If that's what I did decide, I didn't want anybody preventing it. I wanted to be sure what I was doing and not fuck it up.

How much time did we have left in our hour together? Enough to fix this—how I felt? The motor running inside of me too high, too high. The food thing. The darkness in my belly. The way I lay in the bed at night and couldn't sleep. The way I kept replaying the same scenes again and again—the scene in the forest—the sunny leaves on the path. The way David looked when he told me, his face brittle with tears. The time I said I didn't like the way he ate his cookie. The angry look he gave me. The dog disturbed at his feeding. The time he backed his car into mine. *Why did you do that?* I'd asked him. He just looked at me. *You were in the way,* he told me. My license plate was bent a little, there was no real damage, so why did it feel, then at the time, now thinking about it, as if he had punched me?

I could remember all of it and none of it. I got bits and pieces.

My mind searching and searching, running over those same stones. Jostling along in the endless ride over the dark field all alone in the night, the car going too fast and I was at the wheel trying to see where I was going racing over the bumpy terrain. Was there time for all that?

But I said only, "Cheese sandwiches. I can eat those. Orange juice. Sometimes an egg."

"Those seem like good things," she told me. "So you'll have to subsist on those awhile. And, if it helps you, have somebody over for supper, or you could go out."

Yeah, out. Yeah, that'd be fun. Sinclair in winter. The one good restaurant populated by retirees in their good wool pants and lumpy necklaces. I'd go there. Alone? No, she'd said *with someone,* so I dutifully imagined entering the restaurant with various of my friends: Rose in a red quilted jacket, cheeks flushed with excitement thinking it's a little bit like a party. She loved to go out. Listening—again!—to my story in the wooden booth. Nick with a poem to share with me. "Let this be my treat," he'd say.

"It's not enough," I told my therapist fiercely. Suddenly angry at her, because she could just sit there, smug in her marriage. Pictures of her kids on the walls. Smug in her job and her future.

I didn't know her at all. I didn't know what she read, what she thought, who she voted for, what she said to her husband, what her husband was like, how he made love. If he had a certain sound he made, a surprised sound like David used to make. A roar like Brad. A sigh like Thomas. She had these children who adorned her walls but I didn't know what ages they were now, or if they were kind to her or exasperated by her. What was it like being the son or daughter of a psychologist? I had known one or two in my time. Were they healthier? More mentally and emotionally fit? More in touch with their feelings? Was that what my problem was? I had picked the wrong parents.

My mind again seemed unhinged from everything. Racing around and going nowhere. Poking into every drawer, rummaging through the contents. Seeking something, some charm, some talisman, something that would turn everything back, that would make all of this disappear, return me to what my life was before.

I didn't want to think anymore. I had been thinking and thinking for weeks now. The cold dark thoughts of winter and the grinding pain. How could it hurt so much? I didn't even like him that much, by the end of it. But now in my thoughts I reach backward to the man I once loved. The man who delighted me. And that is the man that I miss.

16

The back door slams and I sit up suddenly in the bed. I'm not supposed to be here! Someone's coming!

I've got to get out of here. It would be awful if I got caught. What am I doing here? Am I a prowler?

My only defense is that I took nothing. But in the papers. "Police Beat." An intruder. The whispers in town:

Did you hear what she did?

She went over to his house. Did you hear about this? You know they broke up last year.

Yeah, that's right. Didn't they go together for a really long time?

Yeah—I think about fifteen years. Anyway, he's been seeing someone else.

Who?

That girl Natasha? Something like that. I don't know. She's not from here.

Young?

Kind of. Younger than Virginia.

Well, naturally. So what happened?

Well, what I heard was, Virginia went over to his house when he wasn't there. Went all through his stuff. And then he came home and found her. That's the weird part. She was asleep on his bed.

Was she, like, trying to get him to go to bed with her?

I don't think so. It wasn't like she was naked or something. She was just sleeping.

Weird.

Yeah. I always thought she was a little weird.

I can hear him now, far below, in the cellar. He's coming in. Is he alone? I have to get out of here. But what if he comes upstairs? There's only the one staircase to the second floor. There's no other way out. God. Why did I stay so long? There's no time to think about it. I have to hide.

I hear him in the cellar, hear him coming up the cellar stairs. I have no idea what time it is. It's really dark.

I get up, cautiously, from the bed. Smooth the covers flat, walk backward softly, softly, away from the bed.

His footsteps coming up the cellar stairs. I move quickly, soundlessly, out of the bedroom, pause a moment in the hall. I know which boards creak, how to move in silence in his hallway. I have often slid out of the bed in the morning, moved quietly into the hall, so as not to wake him. I have educated myself in his geography of creaks.

I hear him in the kitchen. There's a glow at the foot of the stairs. He's turned the light on. He is rumbling about in there, checking his messages, rummaging in the cupboards. He wants a drink. He's like a bear down there, rooting around. It could take some time. Good.

I stand silent, frozen in the upstairs hallway, hear him down there, the clink of a glass against another glass, the deeper clunk of bottle against bottle. The sure low glug of whiskey. Good. He sighs. Perhaps he farts, alone, or thinking himself alone, in his quiet house. *Turn on the radio,* I will him. *Make some noise. Listen to some music. Watch television. Check the scores!* Anything to keep him occupied, to keep him in the study, so I can creep down, hide in the dining room, make my way out later, when he's sleeping. But what if he moves through the rooms alone later, glass in hand? Pushing his hand through his hair, talking to himself. A lonely man in the night. A man in his house. Sees the wet gleam of my eyes in the darkened dining room.

What can I do? At any moment he could suddenly decide to come upstairs. I won't have time to hide. I stand upstairs in the hallway, frozen, listening to the silence from below.

Then: "I felt defeated by her," I hear him say out loud.

Upstairs I hear him, his far voice below. In the darkness of the upstairs hallway I mouth the words: *I felt defeated by her.*

By whom? By me? Or by his wife? His girlfriend now? Is he talking about Natalie? Are they through, too?

But how could I—standing here, in my stocking feet, shoes in one hand, trapped in the chilly upstairs of my old boyfriend's house—how could I defeat anyone? I am too defeated myself. Doesn't he know that?

The pale moon shines in through the front windows, leaving a triangular slice of light across the window seat. What should I do?

Should I go down to him, down the stairs, through the dark

dining room with its stern furniture sentinels in the nighttime house?

Should I hide out in his son's old bedroom? Surrounded by his son's stuffed elephants and his granddaughter's crib?

Should I go back into his room, and lie across his bed again and wait until he finds me?

Should I open the one tall window and leap out into the night? That slice of moonlight falling across my falling body as I plummet? But it's two stories down. I could get hurt.

Should I just wait here, motionless, and see what happens?

I don't know what he's thinking, down there in his study all alone. I knew more about him in my imagination than now, when I am with him in his house.

Maybe he thinks he hears a sound upstairs, a stirring. Something up above. A bat caught in the attic? A mouse? It's that darkening time of fall when all the animals come indoors again. When the house at night is full of skitterings and scamperings of small mysterious creatures in the walls. Maybe he's thinking that he'll have to set some traps. I don't think Natalie would like to sleep with him in a house inhabited by others. She'd make a face. She'd wrinkle up her nose. *What's that?* she'd ask him.

And then again, there's something. Not a noise exactly, but a feeling. Of something—someone—in the house with him. If Natalie were here, or someone else, he would put on the brave show, go up to investigate—*to find out what it is,* he'd say to her.

You hear that? cocking his head and giving a listening look.

He'd take the broom, the flashlight, something long, hard, and powerful. He'd go upstairs. Maybe he'd take the stairs two at a time. Show them who's boss—the mice, the bats, the memories.

But he is all alone.

And the house around him must seem so dark and vast and so impenetrable—full of rooms he doesn't enter, furniture he doesn't use.

Maybe he's tempted to go through the rooms, a ghost in his own house, imagines himself moving room to room, picking up one thing and then another—a photograph, a book, a pillow, or a vase.

He must sense my presence. He's not sure what it is.

But he won't come upstairs just yet. He'll sit there by himself and drink his drink. Before going up at last to those dark rooms.

17

I hear his sigh as he sits in his chair, then silence.

The safest thing to do is hide, but haven't we hidden from one another long enough? Haven't we hidden from each other always?

I stop thinking, straighten up, slip on my shoes, and walk downstairs.

The descent to the first floor seems to take forever. Even with my shoes on, I am almost silent. The carpet on the stairs. The thick tan pile pads my footsteps and I make no sound.

Halfway down I stop, hand on the railing, straining to hear some sound from the other room where he is—what? Drinking his drink? Reading his book? Knowing I'm coming? Completely oblivious?

And what exactly am I going to say to him? Should I try to be funny about it? As in: *Oh, hi, I was just passing by and thought I'd sneak into your house and rummage through your drawers while you were out.*

No, maybe not.

Or how about a slightly spooky stance—what if I were to appear suddenly, noiselessly, in the doorway, come upon him unaware. He deep in some book of his or, better yet, staring dismally into space alone in his house at night, depressed, despairing, the sad man alone. He doesn't hear me, doesn't see me. When I speak, quietly, in tomblike tones: *Hello, David.* And then how he starts! He starts up with fear, hand on his heart, as if he's seen a ghost.

So that's another way I could go.

Or maybe, finally, the confrontation. I charge into the room like his own worst nightmare. A raging animal—a stormy gale.

It begins with anger on both sides.

He leaps up from his chair.

Virginia? What in God's name are you doing here? face knotted in his angry way.

But in my fantasy I'm not afraid of him—his doglike posing. *Never mind, David,* I say evenly. *Never mind why I'm here. I think you can guess.*

I like this one, the one where I'm in charge and undeterred by his frail fury. His thin indignation and his pompous rage.

I think you know why I'm here. Because we never did have a real talk about what happened, did we?—you and I.

I sound like a character in an old-fashioned movie. Okay, so what am I wearing? I picture myself in some kind of willowy, stern, yet oddly sexy dress. High heels. Yes. My hair done up in an elegant forties chignon.

And I think it's time we did.

He subsides. He's chastened. I have to give him that. *All right. So what do you want?*

Maybe he sits down now, as if to give me room, but I know it is because my presence there has made him nervous and unsteady. He is afraid he'll shake, or totter, or fall down before my implacable and vengeful glare.

He sits. He sips his amber drink. He looks at me in what he imagines is a steady way, but I know better. I recognize the telltale signs of his nervousness, of his unease.

The little movement of his hands. His jiggling knee.

So? he asks me, with false bravado. This is good, because I don't want him to simply collapse before me. I want just enough resistance so that my eventual triumph feels even more victorious. I want to feel him stiffen against my hands before he falls. I want him to recognize my strength, my greatness. To regret. To rue. To grovel. But not yet. First I want to tell him everything. Everything that I've been thinking everywhere since that night when he dismantled the small, safe house of our existing love.

What I've been thinking in the car, driving along until the road got blurry through my tears, and I had to pull over. What I've been thinking on my walks and walks and walks through snow, through springtime mud, through city streets, through summertime, and through the darkening fall.

What I've been brooding over lying in bed sleepless, going out on wary dates with strangers, trying to keep busy at the office, trying to be part of the world again, abstracted at the bank meetings, lost in thought at the family barbecue, staring away on my friend's sunny porch. *Are you listening to me?* Boring my friends and myself with my troubles again and again. *What he said, what I thought, how could he, why did he, what will I?* All of it. All of it that has burdened me like a terrible weighty knapsack of trouble. Like an endless circling game. I want to tell him all of that. I've told him so many times already in my imagination, even spoken to him out loud as I've been walking, as I've been driving, as I've done my little tasks around the house. Always thinking thinking thinking. But now I want to say it to his face.

But where should I start? I've been waiting for this moment for nearly a year. This moment, when I could say all the things I was too shocked, too confused, too sad to say to him the night he left me.

With a sudden spring in my step I start down the stairs again. Toward the room where he sits waiting for me. He *must* know I'm here.

But he doesn't know that—or anything. He's asleep in the chair with his book on his chest, his mouth open. His head's tipped back on the back of the chair and at first he looks dead. His skin is so pale and unhealthy-looking. I notice how thin his hair is getting; that thick white hair he was so proud of. The book is open, facedown, on his chest—that same book on the Civil War he's been reading for the last two years—and the way it lies there accentuates the bulge of his belly below. In fact, altogether, he looks a sorry sight. Was this what I wanted? Is this the man I've been crying over for almost a year? He's not any of the people I imagined him to be—not the danger-ous, dark-eyed man, not the cruel one, not the dashing one, not the sexy one or the comforting one—he's just a man, aging in the way men age. Moving toward the last part of his life. Disappointed by many things, cheered, a little, by others. Taking his solitary pleasure in his grandchildren, in his books, his music.

He doesn't hear me. He's asleep in the chair with his mouth open. The television is on, but the sound is off.

The room looks different than the room I walked through just an hour before. It looks smaller, shabbier, more crowded with papers and old photographs.

I stand in the doorway looking in at him. He looks old and stupid. Sort of like a fish with his mouth open that way. If I came in now, into this house, into this room, and saw him, without knowing everything I know about him—what would I think? I would think he was some guy asleep in his chair. Some sad lonely fuck alone in his house on a dark September night. A husband, probably, weary with the load of years. Content in the way that husbands can be content, burdened with their burdens, saddled with their wives and children.

I want him to wake up, to see me standing there, to start with surprise and recognition, shock, disorientation. I want to act out one of the many melodramas I've imagined over the long months since our separation; the one in which he grabs me to his chest. The one in which he grovels desperately. The one in which I scornfully reject him. And, of course, the impossible one in which we are reunited.

But he doesn't wake. He's sound asleep.

I used to tease him about that—falling asleep in the chair, in the bed, the light on and the book on his chest, his glasses sliding down his nose. Mouth open.

Sometime during the night he would wake, surprise muffled by sleep, and, if he were downstairs, still dressed, he'd go up, pull off his clothes, and climb into his bed. If he were in bed already, he would take off his glasses, set the book aside, turn off the light, and lie down.

I used to think it was a sloppy act, but now, seeing him here, in his unconsciousness, I realize his bedtime ritual is calculated. Light on, book open, mind tenuously engaged in whatever history, biography, detective novel he is reading. The act is calculated not, as I sometimes imagined, to annoy me, but to stave off the silence and the darkness of his own night thoughts.

I'm surprised by the final feelings I have for him—not anger anymore, not sorrow or longing, not petulance, not irritation, not even curiosity—all that is gone. Instead what I feel, seeing him here, in this small shabby room, is tenderness and pity. He's just a man, after all. He's just a person.

I know he won't wake up. I walk over and stand beside his chair. Standing here, tall above him, I feel an enormous power. I could do anything. I could stroke the side of his face. I could kiss him. I could put my hands around his neck and kill him.

But now, I just want to leave.

I reach down and slowly draw off his glasses. He still has the same pair that he wore the whole time we were together. Gold-rimmed, once fashionable, and somewhat worn—they look too big for him now, or is it that his face has gotten smaller? I fold the glasses carefully and put them on the little table beside him, near his drink. He'll find them without trouble when he wakes. I lift the book off his chest, put the jacket flap in to save his place, and close it. Set the book down on the floor beside him. Then I reach over and turn off the lamp that shines its merciless light upon the lines and shadows of his face.

ACKNOWLEDGMENTS

Thanks to Susan Taylor Chehak, Mary D'Alessandro, Steve Drellich, Betsy Lerner, and Denise Roy for their encouragement and good advice.